T0273377

ZIFT

ZIFT

socialist noir

VLADISLAV TODOROV

Translated from the Bulgarian
by Joseph Benatov

PAUL DRY BOOKS
Philadelphia 2010

First Paul Dry Books Edition, 2010

Paul Dry Books, Inc.
Philadelphia, Pennsylvania
www.pauldrybooks.com

This book was translated with the support
of the National Culture Fund of Bulgaria.

НАЦИОНАЛЕН
ФОНД
КУЛТУРА

Text type: Adobe Caslon
Display type: Futura
Designed by 21x Design
Composed by P. M. Gordon Associates

1 3 5 7 9 8 6 4 2
Printed in the United States of America

Library of Congress Cataloging-in-Publication Data

Todorov, Vladislav.
  [Dzift. English]
  Zift / Vladislav Todorov ; translated from the Bulgarian by
Joseph Benatov. — 1st Paul Dry Books ed.
     p. cm.
  ISBN 978-1-58988-059-7 (alk. paper)
  I. Benatov, Joseph. II. Title.
  PG1039.3.O36D9513 2010
  891.73'5—dc22

                                          2010004233

zift (zĭft) *n.* 1. black mineral pitch, bitumen, asphalt; used as bonding material for road surfacing and, in the past, as streetwise chewing gum. 2. *Slang.* shit. [*Turkish,* from *Arabic*]

December 21,
1963

1

Death solves all problems—no man, no problem.
—Stalin

The story I am about to relate here—to the extent that my dwindling strength and memory allow—began a while back, some twenty years ago. It came to an end last night when I, citizen Lev Kaludov Zhelyazkov, was set free. At the age of thirty-eight, I emerged from the Central Sofia Prison, serving time for murder and robbery. I had been thrown in during one historical period, and I was released into a completely different one; what separated them was the Day of the Revolution, 9 September 1944.

I stepped out of the jailhouse the way many convicts before me have and many after me will—with hope in heart and plan in mind. I had daydreamt much at first, but then I had started duly mapping out the remainder of my life of freedom, before my pointless sojourn on this dumb earth was over and done with.

A Chinese saying has it that a plan is a dream with a target date. My plan was one of the simplest I have ever heard, and it is safe to say I've heard a good many. According to it, after I came out of the Central Sofia

Slammer, I was to make a stop at the Central Sofia Cemetery. From there, the very same night I was to catch a freight train to the Black Sea port of Varna, hide in the hold of a ship, split for the Torrid Zone, settle down on a tropic isle, and swing in a hammock and bask in the sun for the rest of my life.

I planned to visit two graves at the Orlandovtsi cemetery. The first was that of my late son Leo, whom I was destined never to see; he was born after I was thrown in jail. The other was that of the jeweler whose death I didn't cause but ended up doing time for anyway. In that very grave I was supposed to find buried the key to my half-wasted life.

2

I didn't witness how the actual 9 September took place. All I know is that it brought about a simple yet significant change in my prison life, which up until then consisted of sporadic mental growth spurts. Suddenly, the Bible was gone forever and was replaced by *Bakalov's Dictionary of Foreign Words*, which provided in 1949 the Marxist-Leninist definitions of those foreign words previously deemed subversive during the monarchic-fascist regime.

Even the blind could see now that the Dictionary had rendered the struggle against non-Slavic words futile, and I resolutely dove into its pages with the same faith and awe I had earlier granted the Holy Scripture. And, thank God, the Dictionary became a window that opened for me a view of the world as elaborated by Darwin, Tsiolkovsky, Makarenko, and other stellar exemplars of the eternal mind, both collective and individual.

At one point after 9 September, I began to acquire knowledge voraciously and perfect myself both spiritually and physically, inspired by three profound books: *The Gadfly*, *How the Steel Was Tempered*, and *On the Eve*. As part of the process, I started lifting weights and jumping rope. I won second place in the prison's push-ups tournament. I took to reading over and over volume upon volume of fiction and periodicals, with a goal to divine the true nature of things and prepare myself for the moment when I would embrace freedom as an "objective given."

I never prepared for escape and revenge, especially not in my mature period of imprisonment, and unlike my fellow inmates, I read *The Count of Monte Cristo* more as a source of aesthetic pleasure than as a roadmap to life.

I served part of my sentence. My pardon came as a result of my contribution to the implementation of popular education in the daily life of the cooler. More specifically, it came thanks to my propaganda installation "The Communist Time Machine." I put it together with my bare hands, based on my own free will and conceptual design. But it cost me a great deal of effort to find and provide all kinds of badges, painted cast-iron symbols, anthracite lumps, turbine countershafts, flywheels, and other ideologically charged machine parts.

They declared me reformed and let me go. But this inner reform wrecked my nerves. I could build a tower with all the petitions I wrote to all sorts of cultural and industrial institutions, requesting that they provide me with hard evidence of the Communist Time Machine as a topic of meditation capable of rehabilitating the law-breaking citizens. I got the idea for such a propaganda exhibit somewhat unwittingly. It sprang out of me, so to speak, and probably because of that earned me material benefits and, ultimately, freedom.

3

The wall-mounted Wired Radio Outlet at the Central Sofia Joint was feeding songs for the masses through the cool cells. Alexander Stepanovich Popov's invention interrupted "The Triumph of Will and Mortar" in order to broadcast the news headlines, after which "Exact Time" announced the hour. It was 17:00.

I finished my one hundred push ups—an ultimate act of survival in the cell. I shaved as usual, eyes closed. I put on the suit in which they had brought me here years ago. It was an old, stately gabardine, black as a raven's wing, robust in the shoulders and worn glossy in the elbows, "theatrically flamboyant," as the district attorney put it during the trial. I was caught at the crime scene wearing that very garment. I hadn't put it on for twenty years. It definitely looked better on me now because I had grown bigger and I could fill it up nicely. I had bought it specifically for the robbery, as a tool, intentionally big and wide, but more on that in due course.

I shot a glance at the darkened sky beyond the bars, and a fleeting smile must have flickered across my face because I said to myself, "You look at the sky, and it looks back at you with a barred eye."

I took away with me from the cell three things—her letter regarding the death of my son, Leo, the glass eye of my late mentor and cellmate Van Voorst the Eye, and a postcard he owned, which displayed the most sinister and absolutely hypnotic image I've ever seen—a chalk-pale, diabolically rapacious female chewing up a male who'd fallen prey to her, turning his flesh into bloody pulp. I removed the postcard from the wall where it had been hanging for many years, since long before I moved into the cell.

From underneath my mattress, I pulled out an envelope wrapped in disintegrating cellophane, and from the envelope I removed a faded yellowish paper filled with writing—her letter in question, rendered in typically girlish hand. I put the postcard and the letter back in the envelope, and I inserted it in the inner pocket of my gabardine jacket. I straightened out the bed's blanket, picked up the *Dictionary of Foreign Words in Bulgarian*, put its pages in order, grasped it tightly since it was falling apart, and stood waiting by the door to be escorted out to freedom.

The main office of the cooler had a small flimsy "customer" window. There I handed over the *Dictionary*, almost completely loose, and I retrieved the personal belongings that had been taken away from me when I arrived—a large brass key from the apartment with the geranium, in which she and I had lived for a short while;

an old, pre-revolutionary banknote; an indelible pencil; and a chunk of natural unadulterated *zift*.

Next to the window stood a beat-up wicker basket full of rejected personal belongings—handkerchiefs, old coins, keys, worn pocket mirrors, pens, a toupee, garters, mustache dye, and other such material refuse. I tossed my now-useless key and the tsarist money into the basket, but I decided to keep the indelible pencil and slid it into the small pocket of my gabardine. Who knew? Maybe I'd need it both to write with and to use as medicine. They had found the pencil on me at the time of the arrest. Back then, a wart had developed on my little toe. It bothered me when I walked, which wasn't going to help any in the robbery, so I started burning the wart using the indelible pencil moistened with spit, just like a medically savvy barber had instructed me.

I bit at the *zift* and pocketed the rest. I started rolling the *zift* inside my mouth so it would soften. It released its flavor, which slithered through my cranial cavities.

"The end starts at the very beginning." I had hand-picked and memorized this maxim so that I could utter it as I stepped over the cooler's threshold. I wanted to give the moment its due, as it could turn out to be over-whelming, and one might find a bit of wisdom handy in order to stomach it. I couldn't allow this long-cherished moment to simply go by just like that—one foot after the other, and you're out. Walking out, stepping over the threshold, is a special event, like passing under the rainbow and morphing into a completely different person.

Unfortunately, due to some apparent absurdity, at the gate I bumped into the shitty face of a particularly vile warden whom we called the Mole-Cricket. I couldn't help walking past him without smacking him in the mug with the phlegmy curse that had been building up my throat all these years. I expressed myself and left relieved. As for the maxim—I remembered about it only now.

Exact Time announced the hour on the Wired Radio Outlet—it was already 17:30.

4

I walk out into the light of day, so to speak, and all around me spreads a nebulously thick freezing night. The longest night—the night of 21 December 1963. Darkness was crawling along the pavement like some mythical creature, and dusk was streaming down the joint's walls like molten asphalt.

Right in front of me, stealthily, like a hungry tarantula, a shadow flitted.

I froze and the shadow turned into ice—my shadow, my first shadow cast as a free man. It seemed strangely expressive and fantastically dreamlike, its shape affected by the movements of my suit. In that long and massive asphalt shadow of mine, I actually looked awesome, even borderline diabolical.

I stood gazing at myself on the sidewalk of the deserted street, and I was just about to cast one final glance back toward the slammer where my youth was wasted. At that moment of utmost mental intensity, the sudden screeching of brakes disemboweled the darkness and my shadow crumpled. I bristled, as if the night had unloaded its living hernia at my feet.

A Soviet-made Pobeda sedan slammed to a standstill right in front of me. The car was large and unnaturally bulky, something like a giant soap box housing some degenerate life form.

I lean over, meaning to peak in and find out what is going on. At that moment, though, the front door heaves open and a gigantic boot with a lustrous shine thuds onto the sidewalk. In the darkness in front of me, I gradually start to make out the contours of a massive, angular uniformed man coming out of the car.

I don't usually dodge fights, but at that moment something tore inside me and I felt the urge to run. But I was paralyzed by the sheer bulk of the body that disembarked and started unfolding right in front of me. By the look of his dimensions, build, and composition, the man seemed more industrially forged than naturally born. This was some sort of monstrous hybrid between biology and metallurgy—a tin gaze, ears of porous cast iron, a sheet-metal figure, a quarry jaw, skin the hues of zinc and lead, a chest built like a cathedral, a face of lumps and clods, a ramshackle nose surrounded by uneven areas of cheeks, and finally, solid dross under his nails.

After he had completely stretched out in the space around me, this warped entity gave a lumbering salute and trumpeted:

"First Sergeant Varadin Lomski!"

Then he extended a stolid arm toward the handle of the back door, opened it, and wagged a beckoning finger, while his larynx set in motion like a crankshaft, resulting in the following whopping wheeze:

"Citizen!"

I stood there petrified. I didn't dare move. At that moment, Varadin Lomski pulled from under his armpit a rubber baton and executed several finely choreographed wide swoops, slicing up the air around him. Then he raised the baton over his head and brought it thundering down on the car's roof, which resounded like an empty tin barrel. I came to and promptly jumped inside the car.

The first sergeant started moving into the front seat, squeezing in his mega-torso, the car seat loudly crackling. His pate jammed against the ceiling, and he ground his teeth like a corroded hoisting winch. Beneath this human hulk I notice a tiny driver snuggling—a young soldier with a shaved head and a sore red boil on his neck, taut as if he'd swallowed a hose, his arms wrapped around the steering wheel.

Varadin Lomski took a deep breath of air, of all the air, and wheezed out blaringly:

"Report yourself!"

"Private Zaharin Smyadovski!" squealed the soldier high-pitched, clear and loud.

"Private!"

"Sir, yes, sir!"

"Step on it!"

The tires skidded on the ice, then suddenly caught a grip, and the car jolted forward and accelerated smoothly.

"Who are you two?" I say, trying to strike up a conversation.

No reaction, total silence, just the howl of the engine.

"What the devil am I doing in this people's Pobeda?" I raise my voice, hoping for a response.

Then the first sergeant bristled like a wild drake, turned back to face me, drove a crooked hexagonal finger into my chest, and blurted:

"Shut it!"

They turned on the radio and the car filled with popular songs for the masses, praising eternal comradeship, rosy dawns, and sundrenched quarries.

I fell quiet in the back seat and concentrated on the world outside—faces, shop windows, slogans, and other material evidence confirming that while I had been rotting away in the joint the outside world had attained a better state of existence.

Unfortunately, the soldier reeked of some mawkishly obtrusive gaseous compound of machine oil, gunk, and body grime. Varadin Lomski was jouncing up and down, squeezed so tightly in his uniform that his torso looked like it was made of multiple loaves of living matter. At the same time, he was making rhythmic pulsating movements with his jaw and jugular, as if he breathed through gills instead of lungs.

Socialism, whose material bounties paraded in front of my eyes, had induced in me a peculiar state of reverie, when suddenly the first sergeant, while jouncing with his head jammed in the Pobeda ceiling, snapped in a volcanic tone:

"Stop!"

The soldier hit the brakes and his neck strained violently. My body plunged forward uncontrollably, and my nose touched the bursting boil on his neck. I pulled my head back in horror and looked around, trying to figure out where I was.

The car had come to a standstill right in front of the main entrance of the Central Sofia Turkish Baths.

The soldier and the first sergeant jumped out in perfectly timed harmony and opened the two back doors.

"Well played—top score!" I offered sarcastically.

"Get out—as one man!" roared Varadin Lomski.

"I'm all alone. There are no others!" I snapped back at him.

When he heard me, the first sergeant turned a livid green and his face stretched tight, ready to explode.

"Did you bring soap?" I keep up the tune.

The first sergeant's ears filled up with fresh blood. Varadin Lomski was fuming on a molecular level. His temples were throbbing rapidly, as if he were about to change his state of matter. I note the abrupt shift in the physicochemical composition of the inhuman fathead and decide not to bug him anymore. I get out.

Smyadovski started up the steps. I followed after him, prodded along by the oversized Lomski behind me, who at one point blocked the whole entrance with his body and the Baths' main stairwell turned dark.

5

The Wired Radio Outlet at the Central Sofia Turkish Baths announced the Exact Time: it was 18:00. The news filled the air. I try to figure out which direction we'll be headed—inside toward the pool, or downstairs toward the boiler room. We headed downward, and I went so weak in the knees with worry for my personal safety that I staggered forward and leaned against the back of the soldier. I could feel his bulletproof vest.

We descended the stairs and hit rock bottom. We found ourselves in an underworld filled with a viscid darkness.

We walk in the dark. A cadaverously stuffy hallway, putrid air, quivering as if oozing out of a festering crater. A boiler gurgles gaspingly, a light barely seeps in from the far end of the hallway—shivers of pagan horrors creep down your spine.

We stop in front of a galvanized door with a small, filmy window, as if made of old parchment, round like the porthole of an antiquated diving bell.

The door creaked and gaped like an infernal crevice.

"Is this a dream or is it real?" I ask.

"Get in there, you scumbag!" is the answer.

I am shoved into a cramped boiler room. The first sergeant is breathing down my neck. He snaps his fingers and the soldier fetches from somewhere a fuse and a crowbar. They screw in the fuse, and a dim, putrid light envelops the interior of the boiler room, its fixtures emerging in front of my eyes.

Walls, ceiling, floor—all tiled in cheap porcelain, like in some abandoned slaughterhouse. Ungainly, hulking furniture—a table, a bench, a chair. Behind the door, a basin with two large hydrant valves, filled with something like whitish brine, around which are lying a wide hose, a rubber apron, and a pair of rusty forceps. In the corners—tangled pipes, adorned with pressure gauges like the jugulars of a fuming Hydra. A metal cage hangs on chains from the ceiling, and framed in the cage is a massive glass vessel in which a freak strangled with a heating coil is floating freely in alcohol.

Muteness overcame me.

"How can I help you?" I ask, having rallied myself.

"Strip!" Varadin Lomski's voice thunders. "Naked!"

He rammed his foot into the floor and started marching, twisting his heels, two steps forward, two backward, the porcelain around him crunching expressively.

"How naked?" I ask, and despise him.

"Butt-naked!" the first sergeant snapped in two beats and started rubbing the crowbar in his palm, warming it up.

I listened, undressed, and then he blurted the following order:

"Private!"

"Sir, yes, sir!"

"Stop dawdling or I'll bust your skull!"

The solder grabbed my clothes, rolled them up into a ball, saluted, and left the boiler room, saying:

"Requesting permission to leave!"

The first sergeant started circling me just as I was standing there naked and all bristled up. He's staring at me, slapping the bar in his palm, studying my tattoos. He clicks his tongue:

"Tut-tut-tut, scary like in some bloody hell, tut-tut-tut."

"Been there, or you still in it?" I inquire.

He stopped clicking his tongue and went out. The door closed slowly and silently behind him. Someone bolted it on the outside. I was all alone now. Suddenly my eye caught sight of something that disturbed me considerably. It was a very particular curve in the freak's nostrils, as if they'd been cut out. This curve strongly reminded me of my cellmate Van Voorst the Eye, who had a similar, if not that startling, facial peculiarity.

6

During the time we spent together at Sofia Central, my cellmate Van Voorst the Eye was able to paint me all over in ink, in his own image. He collected tattoos himself. He had a few from each of the places where he'd done time. We're talking about whole choreographic scenes: his back was all charted like a pirate's map. But one of these was particularly striking—the one called Centauromachia. It depicted a grand melee of those mythical creatures, part people, part horses.

I tell him:

"You're some spooky sight, man. Tattooed all over like that—not a single blank spot!"

"Being spooky helps. Here in the cooler, if you don't look spooky you're a goner."

"Is that why you gouged your eye out?" I tease him.

"It was an accident, far away overseas! I lost it while ransacking this one estate in Pennsylvania. There was some jewelry stashed away in an old wall clock. I started fiddling with it to get the load out, but midnight struck and the spring shot out and gouged my eye. The whole thing leaked out right on the spot."

"Your skin is like a guidebook, one can tell from it where you've been, and I can see you've been all over."

"The point of tattooing is to depict man's travails. Look," he points at a tattoo, "this eye-tower here was done at the Panopticon."

"The Panopticon?" I ask, puzzled. "The word doesn't mean a prison but a museum exhibit with wax figures of natural phenomena and the greatest examples of human deformity and natural rarity."

"Exactly! It was full, like you say, of the greatest unbelievable depravity. The cooler was a round building, erected around a tall watchtower, no doors, just bars—which makes hiding impossible. Every alcove is visible to the warden, and surveillance becomes all-pervading. Look it up in Bakalov's dictionary."

I really did look it up, and sure enough, according to Bakalov the word's etymology corresponded to the way Van Voorst the Eye was using it. It derives from "pan" and "optics" and means an all-embracing vision, or a gaze that captures everything.

"The gaze," Van Voorst thinks aloud, "is the fastest thing. Once cast, it moves at the speed of light, so in order to hide from it, one needs to exceed this speed, and there is currently no way to do that."

"An optical jail," I say to myself, "how did you like it there?"

"It was educational, but the most interesting part came at the end . . ."

"What was that?"

"As you walk out of there, you meet a sign that reads, 'LEAVE ALL HOPE BEHIND!'"

"Meaning you get out of the cage and you enter the hell of a life of freedom!"

"Meaning that hope is a bird that only flies in the cage, but once set free, it dies."

"Only if you don't have a plan for freedom!" I counter him.

"And you do, do you?" he says somewhat languidly.

"I do."

"What is it?"

"I'll split for the Tropics."

"You never need a sweater there!" Van Voorst is all dreamy, and I add:

"Freedom demands revenge from me here. It wants me to blow out the brains of that creep Slug."

"Once you get there," Van Voorst brings me back to the subject, "you should know that corals are the gentlest formations, essentially living creatures, and when the dirty human hand touches them, they start to die."

"I'll be searching for happiness along the placid shores," I now get dreamy myself. "I'll be searching for peace as exquisitely sturdy as a coral reef."

"Peace, Moth, requires that you sever all ties with people and things outside the cage, especially with women . . . especially with Woman."

I fell silent. I needed time to process the concept. He also went quiet, then added:

"Man is a living coral touched by a woman."

"Ada touched me."*

"Who?"

"Woman, as you say."

"Ada?!"

"Yes, I was in love with her head over heels."

"Ada or Paradise, with a woman you're rolling the dice. Have you heard of this dreadful contraption called a lie detector?"

"Yes," I say hesitantly, "the one where they wire you to a dynamo while interrogating you, and if you lie, you get hit by voltage because the lie turns the dynamo and generates electricity."

"The inventor of this wire, an American, was the author of a comic strip where the main character was a super-female who captured men's secrets with a miraculous lasso and this way rendered them harmless. Later this same comic book author scientifically revisited the artistic idea of the feminine noose and turned it into an electrical conductor of the lie. Peace requires that you sever all wires, conductors, nooses, and female lassos."

I swore to him then to be done with her and when I got out of jail never to look for her—my late son's mother, the woman who made my heart leap like a rabbit's and my mind grow dark when I touched her, as if my stomach were filling up with molten cast iron.

*In Bulgarian *Ada* means "hell"; it is also a woman's name.

As it is clear by now, our plans for a life of freedom were a frequent topic of conversation in the cell. Some time went by, and then I asked:

"What is your plan?"

He keeps silent.

"Aren't you getting out soon?"

"Simple!" he says.

"Tell!"

"There's no telling."

"What's the goal?"

"That I don't get out this time."

"What?"

"Don't ask. It won't get any clearer for you."

He's silent again, then says:

"Moth, I need you to do me a favor."

"For you, anything!"

"When you get out, mail this postcard."

He takes the postcard of the ferocious female off the wall and hands it to me. I'm holding it in my hands for the first time, and I examine it with great interest. It was addressed to a certain Oscar, residing in Vienna. On the back, in faded ink, it read: "Murder is the secret hope of women. For them copulation is a travesty of violation."

"Did you write this?"

"No."

"So who did?"

"The maxim comes from an old Latin book called *The Hammer of Witches*."

"I'll buy it when I get out."

"Be very careful with it!" he says, snickering.

He got out of bed, stood below the cell's window, for a while looked silently somewhere outside into the asphalt night, and then said quietly, as if returning from a distant journey:

"You look at the sky, and it looks back at you with a barred eye."

These were his last words. He hanged himself on the bed frame the night before he was to be set free. I spent the same night crushing rocks in the foundation pit for the Mausoleum, where they were preparing the final resting place for Georgi Dimitrov, the Bulgarian people's leader and teacher, who at the same time was traveling embalmed on the Moscow-Sofia train to serve as eternal dynamo of Bulgarian-Soviet comradeship.

7

I found his eye a few days later in the oddest of ways. Before putting an end to himself, he had hidden it in my mattress. One night I felt it and remembered his saying, "Eyes, Moth, are like peas in the princess's bed—they never let you rest. The more tightly you squeeze them, the deeper you bury them inside your soul, the more they jab you from within."

He would also say that death, unlike freedom, fines us for absolutely no reason. Whatever this cogitation might have meant, to me it sounded prophetic. We later learned that his decision to put an end to his life in the face of freedom had its medical origins. It was called some sort of phobia that occurs due to the coalescence of the human brain with the slammer's workings as a result of internalizing a regime of punishment into the punished's mental balance—or some such scientific mumbo jumbo, which no one paid much attention to.

Van Voorst the Eye's real name was Iliya Aleksandrov Kazandzhiev. As I've already made clear, before doing time together with me at the Central Sofia Cooler, he did time in all sorts of foreign prisons, while criss-crossing the world as a young adventurer in search of diverse challenges, including botanical ones: he had planted, raised, and eaten some kind of narcotic mushrooms and herbs.

It is already known that he had a glass eye that would often pop out, especially when he was boxing. The physical condition and general appearance of that eye weren't appealing. It looked like the broken tip of a discarded billiards cue.

The fact that Van Voorst had lived abroad for a long time made him familiar with a good many foreign words, many more than I myself knew, and I openly envied him for this—a circumstance that pleased him greatly. More than that, he actually spoke entire foreign languages, in which it seemed he was mostly cursing or praying.

Van Voorst the Eye set off to see the world quite suddenly, when he received an inheritance from America and traveled there to sort out the paperwork on the spot. Some distant uncle left him a small amount of money in his will (enough to cover his travel expenses) and a box of very expensive cigars. When he received the cigars, his lawyer advised him to insure them until he decided what to do with them, which he did. When he read the terms of the policy, he discovered to his great surprise that the cigars were insured even against fire. So Van Voorst decides to take advantage of his contractual rights. He started smoking them one after another while wandering around the ports and piers of the East Coast, boxing and picking pockets for a living. This is the time when he loses his eye.

When he finished the last cigar, he filed a claim with the insurance company. He stated in the claim that the cigars had been destroyed in a series of micro-fires, to which there were plenty of witnesses. The insurers brought the case to court, and the court decided in favor of the claimant, relying on the text of the policy. The insurance was duly paid, and Van Voorst planned to open a cigar shop with the money, but all in vain, since he was then arrested. He was prosecuted for arson and sentenced to a whole lot of years, a separate sentence for each fire, to be served consecutively—in the Panopticon.

In any case, he was and remains the person dearest to my heart. When in the summer of 1949 he took his own life, I no longer had anyone either to leave or go back to.

8

Suddenly a tallowy ball of a face smeared itself on the other side of the boiler room's round window—thin teeth, as if filed away, sunk into chapped lips, a shocking nose, brimming and purple like an inflamed cyst. Then all at once the face distended into a meaty smile and winked at me slyly. I recognized it, but something inside stopped me from smashing it with a devastating fist.

The door opened, and the figure of a uniformed man with the epaulettes of a major flared up in the warped frame.

"Slug! You worthless scum!" I hissed through my teeth.

"Stand to attention!" still the same voice—the squealing voice of a gelded school crossing guard.

He makes a hulky entrance, lugging in his corpulent dead weight. He steps unsteadily in misshapen military shoes with battered toecaps and obliquely trodden-down heels. The crowbar shines in his hands. I clutch the bench, as if I am about to lift it and bring it down on top of him.

The treacly silence grew long and syrupy. Slug fixed his eyes on the cage with the freak. He grabbed it in his arms and started winding it around its chain. He let go and it started spinning frantically, like a top. The freak inside is banging against the glass walls, shaking all over, piercing me with an alcohol gaze.

The major whispered, and the silence acquired a voice:

"The diamond!"

"My ass!" I burst out at the top of my lungs in an effort to disperse the hell that had coiled up around me.

"The diamond!" he hissed between widely spaced teeth and poked the bar into my stomach.

He let the iron rod lie in my lap and touch my groin—cold, angular, ready to disembowel me.

"I am looking for it myself!" I cry out and feel the bar starting to twist and prod me like a corkscrew.

"Where did you hide it?" asks the major-inquisitor.

"You hid it!"

"Bullshit!"

"Sir, yes, sir!"

"You are the last one who held it in his hands. I saw with my own eyes how the African remained in your hands after . . ."

"After you shot me and slipped away!" I cut him off and pointed to the bullet scar on my bare shoulder.

The behavior of the crowbar was getting quite ruthless, and it cost me a lot of effort to maintain a fierce look on my face.

"The gem was never found, neither on you nor on the jeweler nor in the safe—nowhere! I personally ransacked the apartment and found a big damn nothing!"

"Yes, I hid it before I even found it," I mock him.

"Yes, you hid it . . . in the walls, in the hardwood floor, inside yourself, somewhere you've got to . . ."

"Search me!" I snarl at him.

I grabbed the bar defiantly as I was sitting naked in front of him, but he instantly snatched it out of my arms, stepped behind me, stuck it into the nape of my neck, and started twisting it as if he wanted to unscrew my skull. I turned sharply toward him and swallowed the pain before his eyes.

"I will search your head!" cried the major.

"Go ahead, dig in!" I challenged him, so he stuck the crowbar into my mouth and I began to choke.

"Here, let me fix your memory coil, because it seems to have short-circuited."

And indeed something back there got unlocked, and the whole vile affair started spinning in my head so clearly, as if on color film. A memory so hot it will melt the celluloid . . .

9

Before I was locked up, I lived on the corner of Nishka and Bregalnitsa Streets, right in the capital's ravenous belly, the area called Yuchbunar. I barely remember my parents. I was very young when my father left for Africa and enlisted in the Foreign Legion. Soon after that, they declared him missing. It never became clear whether the whole enterprise was a pursuit of money and wealth, or if he had run away from us in search of a better life. A year later my mother died of sleeping sickness. Orphaned at an early age, I lived at my uncle's with the understanding that when I turned sixteen I would hit the road like an adult man.

I got the nickname Moth when I was a kid. I was skinny but very wiry and agile. I would hide in pantries and suitcases to scare people. And so it stayed to this day—Moth, because once dubbed, a nickname sticks to you like burdock.

The moth—just imagine how it flies: not flying, really, but zigzagging erratically. If you try to sketch a moth's flight, you will end up with an unintelligible drawing. My life paints a similar picture—anyone's life, really.

Man, as Van Voorst the Eye used to say, is a living coral touched by a sordid woman. Ada touched me. I fell madly in love with her at age sixteen. It was a scorching summer afternoon, at the end of the school year in the junior-high yard. I was sitting on a rickety bench chewing on my *zift* in the middle of the bustling crowd, when all of a sudden a powdery graphitic apparition emerged out of the sweltering heat.

There she was, graceful, fragrant, and tremulous, dangerous like a bud brimming with fulminating mercury. Her body—taut in a diamond-black school uniform with a snow-white collar and a beret; the eyes—hypnotic, their pupils like black crystals, edged by brows of pure asphalt; her breasts—a heavenly fullness, the orifices hewn with a divine tool, her flesh thirsting for flesh. Otherworldly but also earthy, weightless yet imposingly carnal, with a gait celestially languid, almost subaquatic, her tummy thrusting out. Her neck and shoulders conjoined in an exquisite fitting, the crotch invitingly relaxed—an astounding demonstration of an enslaving, unharnessed femininity.

Most striking of all, most virginal yet most sinful, was the lightness of her breathing. Her diaphragm led the most carnal of lives.

She looked around, and as fate would have it her gaze fell on me—whereupon her eyes ignited into infernal bonfires. She approached cosmically ethereal, mercurially nimble, divinely impeccable. She hopped onto the bench across from me, and sat on the backrest, her thighs parted shyly so that I could peep through. Suddenly our eyes met and became entangled.

Then her diaphragm set into motion quite visibly, and her voice—viscous, soft, and thick like plum jam—uttered words that pulled a taut trigger inside me:

"Did you come?"

"I'm all empty," I replied.

I felt relieved, as if I had just discharged a torpedo stuck inside me. This is how our romance began, whose end will follow here.

From an old gypsy woman at the flea market I had purchased a praying mantis in a glass jar so that I could raise at home something living other than my geranium plant. I wanted to buy two mantises to keep each other company, but the gypsy woman warned me that the day would come when one would eat the other, and that put me off the idea. Inside the jar I placed a geranium twig which looked like a mantis. That way, the insect had something to sit on so she'd feel comfortable while praying.

Sometimes I took it out of the jar and let it perch for a while on the geranium so that it could recover its natural sense of freedom. I fed it gnats, moths, and other small insects. I would put it in the sun by the window, and if I watched it long enough as it turned its head like some monstrous human miniature, I would lapse into a strange state of reverie.

I decided to give her the mantis as a token of my mad infatuation. Ada developed a bizarre mystical affinity for the insect. She would say that it was a special creature through which nature was praying to the creator for forgiveness for the Fall of Man.

We decided to get tattoos and went to a barber, an old anarchist and ex-convict, who knew how to do this. I had him draw on my shoulder a night moth; she, a mantis on her tummy, below the navel. After that, she decided to set the insect free.

Moth and Mantis—that's how they knew us among the gangs haunting the canals and playgrounds in the triangle formed by the neighborhoods of Konyovitsa, Yuchbunar, and Banishora. We were madly in love, yet somehow deliberately, and we paraded our love because there was no other couple so striking in said triangle.

For a time we wandered aimlessly and made out in entryways, among mangled trash cans, rickety mailboxes, bloated wall plastering, and rubber loafers on landings. But we got sick of it. Things got gross. It stank of shit and miasmas emanating from the cans overflowing with watermelon rinds and crumpled newspapers that had wiped bottoms.

We decided to rent an apartment so we could make love at will. We needed only minimal hygiene, a regular sex life, and such. She had run away from home because of me. I had been living on my own for a while. My uncle's family had been evacuated to the provinces since it was wartime and all. Besides, I had turned sixteen, and it was expected of me to follow my own way.

My life with Ada led me gradually to drop out of school, and finally I made up my mind to get a job as an apprentice in the turnery of Factory 12, at the time a militarized plant with relatively good pay and free food and clothes.

Another thing—I used to wrestle at the Yunak stadium, ever since I was a boy. I had seen Dan Koloff wrestle free-style, and I realized with time that those who had never seen Dan Koloff fight couldn't claim to know much about life. But despite my fascination with professional wrestling, it always remained a mystery to me. I was neither physically nor mentally set up for the sport. I was tall and skinny and therefore anatomically unfit for a pursuit of that kind, but boxing came naturally to me, which made me rather popular in the neighborhood.

It turned out that combat sports make a woman hot. She would come to watch me so that afterward we could make frantic love, like animals. That was when she told me she was pregnant, which made me go soft. I ripened on the spot.

We began to fantasize about how we would settle in and love each other until we died, but we needed money. At a moment like that, one is ready to engage in all sorts of schemes, including the stupidest ones. We wanted to get married and move away, to seek a new life with new meaning. She sang well, a beautiful voice, and was drawn to the stage. I dreamed about making it in boxing and writing my autobiography in some foreign language.

She quit school and had to start working. That is why we went to see Slug, the neighborhood authority, an older schoolmate—his flesh soggy, smelly, and greasy. He would find people menial odd jobs. He sent her to work for a Russian jeweler named Vladivostok Lyolyushkin, a former White Guardsman and a testy widower, who lived on Maria Louisa Boulevard, above his jewelry store. And all my tribulations were henceforth set in motion.

Slug concocted a plan in which we agreed to take part, realizing full well the inherent dangers. She was going to work for a while at the jeweler's until she made his head spin through feigned naiveté, seduction, and other feminine perfidy. Her mission was to make a copy of the key to the safe. Afterward, Slug and I would sneak into the store on a prearranged night and rob the safe.

The nature of the tasks on which the success of the robbery depended required at least one skilled pair of hands that would deftly handle the safe-cracker's tools. Slug had two left hands, but a creative mind. Fortunately, at the factory I had acquired the needed technical proficiency.

It took some time, about three months, for Ada to completely bewitch the lustful scarecrow Lyolyushkin, and he started having her come over more and more often, even on weekends, so that she would do various chores around his house. Soon she made an astounding discovery that would change our plan. We called Slug to discuss the situation. It was the end of the summer of 1943.

10

Languid afternoon swelter filled the deserted streets of Yuchbunar. We met as usual at uncle Tymé's neighborhood sweetshop. I arrived first. The tree on the street cast a thick shadow over the table by the shop window, and I sat there. White oil paint on the window read WAF-FLES, SEEDS, LEMONADE, AYRAN, BOZA, and other confectioneries.* The hardwood floor freshly mopped and smelling of bleach, recently whitewashed walls, everything neat and sanitary.

There was no one inside. Uncle Tymé was dozing behind the counter and muttered something as I walked in. He then lumbered over in his clattering clogs to bring me a large glass of ayran—my usual order—and sank back into his afternoon slumber. I drank half the glass in one gulp, then started to chew on my *zift* and loaf around.

---

*_Ayran_ is a cold drink made of yogurt, water, and salt. *Boza* is a thick, sweet Balkan beverage made from fermented barley or other flour, which contains a minimal amount of alcohol.

Suddenly Ada's figure emerged out of the street haze. She passed in front of the shop window, phlegmatically crossed the threshold and sat beside me, sipped from my glass, glanced at me, passed an agile tongue over her lips, and said:

"Give me."

"What?"

"Ayran."

"Which one?"

"The white, tart, thick one."

"Mine."

"Yours I know."

"You're looking for another."

"Still looking."

She reached for my glass with a slender arm on which jingled three bracelets I had given her. She drained the glass, as if sponging up the ayran with her whole body, and licked the tip of her lips salaciously.

"How does it go in?" I ask and give her a wink.

"Coolly. It quenches my heat!" she winks back.

I grabbed her arm and sharply pulled her toward me. She coiled like an eel, fell over me, started to kiss and lick me, to jounce as if her fist-tight butt was churning butter in my lap.

Suddenly Slug's slimy face glued itself to the window and trickled down like warm galantine. Ada saw him and something curdled inside her—she tore herself free from my embrace and sat on the other chair. Slug came in, bought a bag of sunflower seeds, and then sat

38 | ZIFT

next to us. As he spoke, he started cracking the seeds, spitting out shells everywhere.

"What's up now?" says the snotty bastard.

"There is a second safe!" she says.

"Ha!" he grunts. "Where?"

"Built into the living-room wall, behind a hanging rug with a galloping camel on it."

Slug rubbed his greasy forehead and concluded:

"Makes sense! The more safes, the smaller the risk that one day you'll be completely cleaned out."

"Yes, but the Bijou," that's what we'd started calling Lyolyushkin, "has only one safe key on his chain," Ada says and looks out through the shop window.

"Probably both safes use the same key," I chime in.

"Meaning that the loot doubles," says Slug.

"No, just a key won't open either safe."

"What then . . . aha, the code!"

"Yes, 'cause the Bijou first enters the code and then turns the key, right?" I ask her.

Ada nods but keeps staring out the window.

"The two safes probably use different codes."

"Meaning what?" asks the gaping Slug.

"The code mechanism can be forced open with a special tool."

"Do we have it?"

"No, but I can make it at the factory."

"Hold it, hold it," he says. "Let's think . . . One key for two keyholes, one tool for two codes, therefore we can attack both safes."

"Like hell you can!"

"Why not?"

"A double hit requires double time," Ada says languidly, without even looking at us, as if uttering some platitude.

"We can only do one safe!" I say firmly.

"Which one?"

Slug asked the question and started spitting shells from a handful of seeds he had thrown in his mouth at the beginning of the conversation.

"Time will tell," she said and got up to leave, tugging my leg under the table.

We parted from him without an answer to the central question, but in anticipation of some hint. And that hint came. We met with him again one Friday at the same place, only it was already late fall and the leaves had dropped from all the trees.

11

"The most valuable item," Ada opens the meeting, "is not in either safe but out in the open."

Slug stares at her silent, waiting to find out where.

"On top of the cabinet," she adds.

"Makes sense!" Slug says in his familiar manner. "As though there is nothing of special interest . . . So what's the item?"

"A diamond," she says, and he squeals like a eunuch.

"A diamond? Don't kid around!"

She nodded her head.

"How did you find out?"

"A strange gentleman showed up this morning on some extremely important and confidential business. I eavesdropped on their conversation."

"And?"

"I didn't hear everything," she went on, "but I think I know what's going on."

"Spill the beans!" Slug was growing more and more impatient.

"They were talking about an expert evaluation of an exceptionally precious diamond, custom-made for some foreign private collection. Then the Bijou said that on Monday he'll close the store early so that he makes it to the bank before the end of the business day."

"Most probably," I speculate, "the diamond will be escorted to a safe deposit box."

"Makes sense," says Slug, "at the end of the business day."

"And why does it make sense?"

"That's when there are the fewest loafers on the streets and in the bank."

"What do we do?" she asks somewhat irksomely.

"What do you mean 'what'—we attack the escort!" Slug says.

"The three of us? . . . You must be kidding!"

"The hit should take place before the escort arrives," she suggests.

"All right," says Slug pensively, "then you have two days until Monday to secure an imprint of the key. If the diamond doesn't turn up, at least we'll rob the safe."

"And how is this supposed to happen in two days?"

"With a little charm," says the bastard and winks at her. "Dangerous, enslaving charm . . . You'll mount him if you have to."

"Why don't *you* mount him!" I grab him by the sleeve.

"Stop it!" She pulls me back.

Silence sets in. I chew on my *zift*. She looks out the window and shakes one leg, then smiles and delivers the following news about the jeweler:

"Even if you want to, there is nothing to mount."

"What?" Slug is at a loss.

"Vladivostok Lyolyushkin doesn't have a cock."

"Yeah, right, stop shitting me!" Slug waves a finger.

"I'm not shitting you. He owned up to it himself."

"Impossible. How?"

"Here's how. His mother gives birth to him in Odessa and comes back home with him from the delivery room. His five-year-old sister sees him naked for the first time while he's being swaddled and asks what that thing is hanging between his legs. They tell her it's a growth that the doctors forgot to cut off. The next day, while the mother is kneading dough, the little sister takes a pair of scissors and removes the 'growth.'"

"Lyolyushkin, the Odessa eunuch!" Slug chuckled, but didn't seem to buy the story and went up to the counter to get more seeds.

"Seeds . . . H-e-e-e-y, uncle!" the bastard bleated.

"Huh?" Uncle Tymé started up from his nap.

"Seeds!" and he threw a coin on the counter.

Uncle Tymé handed him a bag of seeds and said:

"It must be real hot in Africa right now."

"Stop talking nonsense and go back to sleep," he cut him off over his shoulder.

He came back, started chewing and slobbering, then spat in his hand and said:

"This story sounds lame—I've heard it told about other people."

43

"Be careful it doesn't happen to you," I growled.

"I'm always careful." His face turned serious. "Where exactly is the diamond?"

"In the penis of a naked African boy with a protruding belly and a spear in his hand," she says laughing, "an African figurine."

"Poppycock!" he looks at her furiously, and she snaps back:

"For real! Ever since the figurine arrived, the Bijou has been watching me closely while I clean the living room, doesn't let me touch it . . ."

"How big is it?" Slug interrupts her.

"Just shy of a foot tall."

"And the penis?" he asks and spits.

"Just shy of half a foot."

"Excessive . . ."

"Massive," she adds.

"Is it heavy?"

"Quite."

"So how come the African doesn't tip over?"

"It does."

"So he's hiding something inside."

"That's what I'm saying."

"It could be sloppy craftsmanship."

"I don't think so. The other day I picked it up to dust it," she glanced through the shop window and went on in a listless manner. "The penis turned out to be detachable—it twisted as if it was screwed on . . . When he saw me, the Bijou bristled and snatched it out of my hands. He claimed it was an extremely precious item and I should never, ever touch it. Today, as I was eavesdropping on the confidential conversation with the jewelry expert, it dawned on me that they were meeting about the African."

"Let's pinch it!" Slug suggests.

"Yeah, let's go for it," I nod affirmatively.

"But how?"

"Here is how." I lay out my idea: "The figurine is on the third floor of a five-story building. We enter through the kitchen window, which faces the back yard. Ada will crack it open before she leaves."

"The yard is deserted, cluttered with crates from the grocer's," she adds.

"Good thinking," he says, "but this means we have to clamber up the outside wall."

"We'll go down a rope from the roof," I correct him.

"Through the attic," she says, still gazing out the window.

"We go up there in the morning, before dawn, so nobody sees us."

"During the day, police patrol the street. He pays them to do it," Ada says.

"We'll crouch there all day?" Slug frowns.

"Until nightfall."

"So we go into the apartment through the kitchen window?"

"Yes!" she snaps. "Think! You're the expert, aren't you?"

"How do we get out?" he asks.

"That's the question!" I shoot him a look. "Climbing back up the rope would be hard, going down the stairs—dangerous."

"So," he was suddenly quiet and then continued, "we jump out the window into the yard."

"From the third floor?" she asks puzzled.

We're silent. He's munching on a handful of shells, I on my *zift*. She drifts away somewhere beyond the shop window, and I see that she's growing tense.

"Yes!" Slug cries out. "We jump with the mattresses from the beds straight onto the crates, and then over the fence and we're at the other side of the square. We'll get oversized old suits from the flea market. We'll stuff them with wadding so we land softly as we hit the ground and don't kill ourselves."

"If you say so . . ."

12

The Sunday before the hit, while scrubbing the mosaic by the apartment entrance, Ada managed to get the imprint. Vlad Lyolyushkin was about to unlock the door on his way out when he gets an urgent "call of nature." He races to the toilet and leaves the bunch of keys hanging in the lock.

The key was duly made and the hour of the robbery set. Before daybreak Slug and I went up to the attic. In a backpack we carried tools, suits, wadding, thick rope, and gloves to prevent our hands from blistering and from leaving fingerprints. We tied the rope to one of the attic girders, stuffed the suits with the wadding, and decided on what each of us would carry. Then we settled in for a long and tedious wait. We had nothing to say. We could barely stand each other. We sat quiet, chewing. He— seeds, I—*zift*.

Before she left the apartment, Ada was supposed to make sure the figurine was in its place and to unlatch the kitchen window without being noticed by Lyolyushkin, who always personally saw her out and locked the door behind her. After leaving the building she was supposed to whistle a certain tune so we would know if everything was okay. We had come up with one tune for "go" and another for "no go."

As I squeezed the lump of *zift* in my hand, I was filled with premonitions. The Alexander Nevsky Cathedral struck five o'clock. From down below came the tune "Where are you, faithful people's love," which meant "go." Slug and I crawled out through the roof skylight, looking like mournful clowns, dressed in the huge black suits. I tucked the *zift* away, and we unwound the rope. I descended first, he followed me. Now I understand that before going down he wanted to see if the rope could hold me.

I gave the kitchen window a light kick and it swung open. I jumped inside and headed straight for the living room. My flashlight roamed the furniture and walls. My attention was drawn by a whole collection of grotesquely demonic cast-iron toys arranged in the cupboard. Suddenly, from behind one of the cupboard glass-cases, the African boy flashed before my eyes—right under my nose. The glass slid easily, and I reached inside and grabbed it.

I was turning the figurine in my hands, appreciating the penis in question, when the apartment door suddenly opened. I turned off the flashlight, but apparently too late. The door slammed, and almost immediately Lyolyushkin's paunchy silhouette darted into the dim room. An electric switch clicked and bright light poured over me. I froze, blinded like a rabbit caught in the head-lights, and a scream pierced the air:

"To stop, you scoundrel . . . I to shoot . . . hands up . . . The Lyolyushkin you maraud not to dare!"

Just as my eyes are adjusting to the light, I make out Lyolyushkin feverishly trying to pull out his pistol, which had gotten entangled in his pocket. Right then Slug charged into the room and pounced on him. But the jeweler was no joke because instead of retreating he counterattacked by headbutting Slug so hard that he knocked him out cold on the floor. Lyolyushkin emerged from the tussle pistol in hand, and the pistol was pointed at me. He was about to roar something at me when suddenly he himself collapsed as if his legs had failed him. Slug, lying on the floor, had kicked him in the shins. The gun flew off to the side, scattering the cast-iron toys like billiard balls, breaking the cupboard glass-case.

The two bodies lunged forward in a deadly grip, but Slug got to the cupboard first and the pistol gleamed in his hands. Then came a shot and the jeweler fell prostrate and started gurgling like a slaughtered animal—a maddening sound, which soon alternated with massive wheezes.

Suddenly, to my utter astonishment, I see that the filthy swine is pointing the gun at me, and he says:

"Give me the African."

"Are you mad?" I yell at him, and he squeals:

"Throw it to me, or I'll blow your brains out!"

"Come get it!" I hiss at him.

His eyes opened wide, he blurted some garbled string of sounds, and then he fired. Something extremely massive, like a fireball, hit me in the shoulder, and I staggered backward. An agonizing pain gripped me, but I managed to stay on my feet and even advanced in my rage, meaning to waste the scumbag. He must have gotten scared because he tried to shoot again but the gun misfired. He pulled the trigger again but the gun misfired once more. I took a vigorous step forward. He also headed toward me but suddenly stopped. He probably decided that he wouldn't be able to overpower me, despite the bullet he had plugged me with. And he was right—at that moment I was ready to obliterate him, to absolutely and fanatically spit in his lungs, to scatter his brains with the very hand now writing these lines.

Just then there was knocking on the door, which turned into wild banging combined with muffled shouts. Slug debated what to do, but not for long. He threw the pistol at me and ran toward the kitchen. I managed to catch the gun in the air and darted after him, writhing in pain. I caught a glimpse of him jumping out the window and that was it—the night swallowed him and I never saw him again. I cursed him profusely and returned to the living room, where I found myself alone with the jeweler, whose wheezing was growing weaker, like a fading satanic giggle.

I started to pray.

They were already breaking down the door with pickaxes . . . sounds of splintering planks, wheezing, and a screeching in my ears. Pistol in one hand and an ivory African in the other, I leaned over Vlad Lyolyushkin, who by this time was turning blue. I heard the gun drop to the floor in front of me, and then somehow, mechanically, my fingers unscrewed the penis, and lo and behold, something massive, hard, and angular settled in my palm.

I look down, and what do I see—an exquisite black carbonado diamond.

13

I n an effort to snap me out of my reverie, the major
neighed in my face, in a distorted falsetto:

"Sing and you live, or else you soak in alcohol!"

"I have no song to sing!" I develop the metaphor,
but he strikes a heel in the floor, his nose fluffy like Eas-
ter babka.

"You're lying! When Lyolyushkin saw you holding
the African, he went berserk. Otherwise, why would he
risk fighting masked thieves just for a hollow savage with
a spear?"

"You're forgetting the safe."

"So?"

"Nothing . . . He catches us, he's carrying a gun—it
makes him brave—so he goes after us."

"Right after they find you, the police find the African lying at the scene of the crime with an unscrewed
penis. Had the penis not been unscrewed, then maybe
we were wrong, maybe there was no diamond in it. But
somebody must have unscrewed it!" Comrade major
slaps the crowbar in his palm and wriggles below the
waist. "It must have been you. Who else?"

By way of emphasis, he jams the bar into my ribs and repeats:

"Who else?"

I doubled up in pain and barely uttered through my teeth:

". . . there was no diamond . . . I jumped out of the window right after you . . . I dumped the figurine and jumped because they were already coming in. So what if the penis was unscrewed? Screwed, unscrewed . . . I tell you, it had no diamond."

"Damn it, Moth! Stop bullshitting me because I can make your life hell. Don't provoke me! Don't! I can damage you physically and mentally."

With the crowbar, he banged on the metal door and then roared to out-shout the thundering echo.

"Wine!"

Practically that very second, as if long ready, the first sergeant came in carrying a tray—a pitcher of wine, a round loaf of bread, yellow and white cheese, grapes. He laid this cornucopia on the table in front of me, saluted, and went out. My stomach turned over and started howling like an animal in heat. Only then did I realize that I was starving.

"Eat . . . go ahead . . . drink, stuff yourself!" the major urged me.

So I stuff myself. I drain one glass of wine, then another, and go on gorging. Slug just watches me, not touching anything—not the grapes, not the wine. He comes closer, smirking in my face:

"Why didn't you rat me out?" His nose stinks of puss.

I lost my appetite! I stopped chewing and fixed my eyes on the freak, who was drowsily quiet in his natural habitat.

"It's obvious," I say. "So that it looked like I was acting on my own. If I had turned you in, you would have framed her. This way no one found out there were others besides me. There was no way for them to find out if I didn't tell, and even if I had, I was already in, with or without accomplices."

"Noble!"

"I wasn't protecting you, but her and the child—she was pregnant with Leo. Because of Leo—so that he wouldn't be born in jail—you, Slug, escaped."

"So—not for Slug, but for her!"

"Sir, yes, sir!"

"Don't you want to ask about her?"

"No!"

"Why not?"

I paused, then stretched out my arm and gave him the finger.

He turned his back to me and grew quiet, somehow full of suggestion. It was as if a heavy curtain had fallen and we were at intermission.

I was breathing heavily, expecting to find out what the silence meant. He started to pace back and forth, dragging the crowbar behind him and listening to it rattle on the cement floor. Then he stopped suddenly, turned around sharply, and left the boiler room.

Some time went by, during which I was able to mull over my situation. I decided to wait for the opportune moment to split. The outside world offered various possibilities, or so I thought then.

Suddenly he burst back into the room, as though he'd broken in. He started pacing again in the fashion I've described. Then he suddenly stopped and started speaking slowly below his breath.

"You're doomed!"

"How banal. Try again."

"I doomed you. I did."

"Moira in epaulettes!"

"Enough babble!" Thick slobber sputtered out of the major's mouth.

He sniffled furiously, swallowed audibly, and brought the bar down with all his might onto the freak's cage.

"You're poisoned, you fool!"

"Poisoned?"

"Poisoned, yes! And you're shitting around . . ."

"Bluffing again."

"Bummer, wrong guess! The wine was poisoned."

"That's moronic, comrade major. You're talking out of your ass. Why don't you use it to perform a patriotic song instead."

"Profaning the people's anthems . . . You're forgiven 'cause you're an idiot."

I stuck a middle finger in his face again, but he ignored it and said:

"Open up your ears and pay attention—a moment ago you consumed enough poison to finish you by morning. Slow but certain poison."

"And what did you have to poison me for?"

"Listen closely."

I became all ears.

"There is an antidote for this poison. But it's in the hands of the one who administers the poison—me!"

He fell silent, as if waiting for his words to take root in my brain, and then he went on:

"If you tell me now where you hid the stone, you leave this death chamber alive and well. In other words—I give you back your life. If you don't believe me, you stay here until you do, until you start writhing, foaming at the mouth, and raving."

He slowly stood up and stepped back. Then he grew quiet and hissed:

"And no stupid tricks. You have no chance of getting out—my boys will break your neck. The bathhouse is guarded on all sides."

The door opened and he disappeared into a ball of sulfurous fumes spiraling down the hallway. An order resounded, and the door was bolted.

I found myself all alone with the freak, swaddled in a shroud-like stench. I reconsidered the situation and concluded the following: I was doomed. Even if I told him, or whatever I told him, diamond or no diamond, he was going to let the poison do its work, for a very simple reason—I knew the terrible truth about him, that he was the murderer. He killed the jeweler with his own hands, and then tried to shoot me, the only witness. And it wasn't exactly clear how the people's authorities would look upon a belated but shocking confession on my part.

I could potentially do him more harm than the diamond good. And in his efforts to get one, he needed to be rid of the other. In short, Slug was right. I was doomed—poisoned or not. I was doomed from the moment I set foot outside the cooler gate.

Quite some time must have passed without my realizing it. I was deeply engrossed in solving the central question of my life, and I was sitting thus engrossed when I began to feel nauseated.

"The poison!" I whispered to myself.

14

"**G**et up!" someone jabbed me in the ribs and I rose.

The voice sounded almost as if it came from the hereafter, as if from a barrel. I turned around and saw a brawny *tellak*.* I knew he'd started working on me because my skin was on fire. A burning sensation engulfed me completely in its own magical way and opened in my head some hidden door leading back in time, many, many years back, when I used to come here with my father. Those are some of the few memories, if not the only ones, I have of him. He would hold me in his lap while the *tellaks* scrubbed me with their stinging *keses*. Back then, this was considered consummate bliss, and the bath was a happy holiday for the body.

But the holiday ended and pain seized my skin. The *kese* was biting, as if made of coarse sandpaper. I tried to tear myself away, but the *tellak* pushed down hard on me, put me in a half-nelson, and went on scrubbing more and

---

* A *tellak* is a public bath attendant, or masseur, who scrubs clients' bodies with a coarse bath mitt called a *kese*.

more fiercely. I clenched my teeth and started gathering strength to break loose, but suddenly:

"Moth!" the *tellak* burst out, nearly rupturing his windpipe.

He was staring dumbstruck at the moth tattooed on my shoulder, then he grabbed me by the neck with the *kese* and fixed his eyes on my face. I look at him too and can't believe my eyes—Raicho the Skin. That's what we used to call him back in the day. His father was a *tellak*, and now I find the son in the same line of work. We were great, inseparable friends, and that friendship of ours caused some major trouble. We were antsy, we spent our days along the canals, and in the evening we would hang around the windows of the women's section at the Baths to feast our eyes on bathing nudity; we would smoke cigarette butts, and in the winter we set fire to piles of car tires; we would grope gypsy girls under the bridges and read the Brothers Grimm. He had Snow White and the Seven Dwarfs tattooed on his back and became the idol of all the neighborhood kids. We were growing up carefree until one day Raicho disappeared. Gossip spread that the gypsies had kidnapped him to get him married to some beauty who he had had sex with under the bridges. Then it turned out that they hadn't kidnapped him but that he'd run away to them himself when his father banished him because of the affair. I was his best man at the wedding, and I never saw him after that.

I was nearly speechless. "Raicho!" I exclaimed, while he says:

"You're in deep shit, best man—very deep!"

"What are you supposed to do to me?"

"Scrub you raw and throw you into this bath of vinegar and salt."

"So now what?"

"Beat it, man!"

"Where to?"

"At the end of the hallway there's a sheet-iron door. That's where they pile the coal for the furnaces. Climb up to the boiler room trapdoor and you're out."

"Got it!"

"Hit me, so the guards won't suspect anything . . . Hey—in case you still care—you'll find her in the joint on Malko Turnovo Street."

"Malko Turnovo?"

"That steep alley behind the palace . . . Come on, hit me, but hard, so they believe it."

I hit him soundly across the face with the bench and busted his mouth. He squealed like a stuck pig, spat out a bloody wad of phlegm, threw himself at me, and knocked me to the floor under the legs of the guards, who were already rushing in. In trying to separate us, they fell to the floor themselves and all hell broke loose. Suddenly, the Skin locked his legs around Varadin Lomski's neck and held him for a moment while I managed to crawl out from under the melee. I jumped to my feet, grabbed the crowbar, which was lying there, and used it to bolt the door from the outside.

I start dragging along the hellish corridor toward the light seeping through. I bang into a sheet-iron door. It cracked open and I peeked around—inside it was empty, a bare bulb shining faintly, the walls crooked, plastered with newspaper cutouts, portraits of men in suits, scenes of jubilant crowds and of gymnasts bearing flags, and in the corner—a heap of dirty sheets and an enormous barrel, where wooden clogs were soaking in a greenish-blue disinfecting solution.

I'm standing naked in the roaring boiler room. On one side, a woman gapes at me, rather gnarly and crotchety, clacking her jaws and wriggling her hips. A pair of pink bloomers and a vest-bra made out of canvas is drizzled on her. She's wringing out a thick hemp rag in a cast-iron tub, looking like a flabbergasted crocodile and batting her eyes.

I grab a sheet from the pile, jump behind a column, and hectically wrap myself in it, while she shakes her blubbery flesh in a guttural laugh and flings the wet rag at me, which splatters on the column and slowly slides down like a giant Turkish soufflé.

I pinch a pair of clogs from the barrel, put them on, and then fling myself deeper into the bath's crypt toward the heap of coal. I notice high up on the dark boiler-room ceiling the metal trapdoor. Dim artificial light seeps in around its hinges. I start scaling the coal, scrambling upward with arms and legs, while a suffocating avalanche of dust slides down on me. I make it to the trapdoor, open it, jump out, and start shaking off the dust that covers me. Then follows a bout of hacking coughs—the lungs, clogged with dust, started writhing, not letting me be. A quiet, neon night and a freezing cold spread all around me. I hear passers-by walking and talking.

I stumbled along the bath's outside wall like a homeless sleepwalker, looking for a way to get back inside without being observed. I needed my clothes—I wasn't going to get very far draped in a sheet and clacking along in clogs. Luckily I notice a window whose warped sash is ajar, the din from the baths pouring out. I climb up the gutter, which God seemed to have wrenched down just for me. It was a good thing I was wearing clogs, otherwise I would have torn my feet. I bang into the window and it opens wide. The sheet gets caught in the gutter, my body leans forward, and stark naked, once again, I fly inside, not knowing where I'll find myself.

I meet the floor with my heels, the clogs slide sideways, but I manage to keep my balance. I charge forward amid gaping mouths, white unctuous flesh, and the echo of falling water, thinking that I'm bound to fail. The mass roar of a frenzied crowd resounds and reverberates against the walls. I disappear among soggy torsos and everything grows quiet. All around me, *tellaks* girdled in waistcloths are toiling, bodies are submersed in cumulous steam, swathed in a faint light, black *keses* scrub backs and shoulders, spools of grime spew forth, and the male sex groans heavily like a chased hedgehog.

The Wired Radio Outlet fed the bathhouse with Danube folk dances, while I, huddled in a shower stall, was about ready to capitulate. Just then, a powerful jet of ice-cold water blasts me and flings me against the wall. I try to resist, but the jet knocks me down and pushes me along the floor like the most wretched piece of garbage.

All of a sudden everything grew quiet. Some time passed. I look around dazed—the bath is deserted, as if evacuated. I lie on the floor, and above me hovers a voice that says:

"Happy bath, you filthy Moth!"

Varadin Lomski emerges before my eyes and delivers a polygonal fist to my face, then ties me across the chest with a thick fire hose and starts dragging me along the wet floor, all the while talking:

"Where do you think you're going, boy? . . . You're running, trying to get away! . . . Slipping away from the long arm of the law . . . For folks like you only the forced-labor madhouse will do."

They stuffed me into my clothes. Wet as I was, they shoved me back into my suit, as if it were a straitjacket. They brought me out back and threw me into the car. Next to me, Varadin Lomski smelled odd, probably a side effect of the poison. I had read that poisons alter one's sense of smell, make people hallucinate, have visions of both shapes and smells. Nonetheless, the first sergeant's armpits really reeked of soap made of processed carrion.

15

The Pobeda came to a stop at the main entrance of the Poduyane train station. Lomski, the construction crane that he was, dragged me out peremptorily, then scooped me under his arm and set off. I sensed Smyadovski breathing down my neck from putrid jaws, and I wondered what exactly the soldier was up to right behind my back. It was obviously some routine for escorting prisoners.

They took me into the waiting room, set me on a long bench, and settled down on each side of me. Inside, the station was cold and dreary, the platform hazy and desolate. The clock struck seven-thirty. Two hours had gone by since I set foot outside the cooler's gates, and now here I was, at this dumb station, when according to my plan I needed to be in a very different place.

"Right on time!" Varadin Lomski noted and bit into a poppy seed roll.

He had just stuck half of it in his mouth when a scraggy gypsy woman emerged from the dark, dandling a baby and wriggling as if her hips had come unhinged, and uttered in a tobacco-stained voice:

"Comrade boss, give us a chunk to eat, spare us a lev or two,* 'cause we need to get us some milk for this here guzzler Tseko Tsekov."

Then she suddenly tossed guzzler Tsekov into Lomski's lap—a specific part of the first sergeant's body, which at that moment appeared as massive as a geological formation, offering what seemed to be a gigantic crib.

"Here! You and the guzzler get lost . . . Clear out, I tell you, before my shit boils over!" the first sergeant gurgled with his mouth full.

The gypsy woman grabbed in panic the piece of roll in one hand and the swaddled Tseko Tsekov in the other, and some invisible broom swept her back into the dark.

The train approached the platform drowsily, snorting like an iron stallion, engulfed in a white cloud of steam and frost. The wheels screeched piercingly and it came to a halt. Nobody got off and nobody got on, except the three of us. Zaharin Smyadovski opened the car door and nimbly jumped inside. I scrambled up after him despite the pain growing in my joints. Finally Varadin Lomski stuffed himself into the aisle, in consequence of which the handle on the toilet door gave in, something broke, and the door flew open. The can took in a not insignificant portion of the sergeant's anatomy, which in turn displaced outward an equivalent volume of sour air.

*The *lev* is the currency of Bulgaria.

Lomski tried to pull in his stomach so he could shut the toilet door and stop the outflux of the stench. But the train suddenly jerked, first setting off, then sharply stopping, and then moving forward again, like a horse throwing a massive kick. The sergeant's head resounded like an empty tin can as it hit the wall, and he doubled up, got stuck in the lavatory's doorframe, and roared thunders. The soldier collapsed at his commander's feet, then turned as pale as a sheet, and started snuggling, fussing, and tugging him by the belt with all his might.

Luckily I was the only one to keep my balance and was still standing upright. Just then, without batting an eye, and somehow automatically, I opened the train car door across the aisle and flew out like a projectile. I landed on my butt and rolled into a ditch. I watched the train slowly plow through the dark fog and saw two black bodies fly out of it cursing. I jumped up and darted off, with both of them on my heels. I could hear their legs digging through the gravel and gradually catching up to me. I knew very well where I was headed, and my goal suddenly materialized before me—the Vladaya River canal, sprawled out in the dusk like a cross-sectioned proboscis.

I jumped in without a second thought, tumbled down the stone embankment, and set out toward the Lions Bridge. I realize at one point that I'm not so much running as dragging along. I didn't have much strength. I was feeling nauseated from the smoky fog and the smell of shit. I had no traction and was drifting forward like some frayed kite. I suddenly stop and hear rumbling—large, heavy boots thumping, and something else, something like a flimsy scurrying accompanied by sporadic hacking.

I took off again, lunging forward as hard as I could, my legs giving way like flabby macaroni. I was moving forward in jolts, but then I started to feel sick, to lose my bearings and get dizzy. The poison was definitely having its sway. The head heavy like a barrel of pickled cabbage, the brain knocking about in it and diving indiscriminately.

All of a sudden I see the canal bed bifurcate like in a biblical scene. "I'm getting close to the neighborhood," I told myself and stopped so I could look around and make sure of it. But suddenly a figure flitted up in the bushes on the bank. I recognize Smyadovski and turn around only to see Lomski's body swell up out of the dark, ready to jump on me. I furiously lunge ahead along the left branch, which makes a turn toward the gypsy neighborhood.

Charging forward like driven cattle, I sense that I'm starting to expire, until I see a streetcar going over a bridge a block away. "Hold on," I say to myself, "you're almost there!" And with a great effort I claw up the canal's stone wall. I make it to the top and huddle under the bridge so I can surprise my pursuers.

Smyadovski arrives first and starts bustling about like a headless chicken when I jump out of nowhere, topple him to the ground, grab him by the throat, and hiss at him to be still or I'll pluck his head off like a fly.

I hear Lomski's lumbering approach, and like a steel caterpillar he starts crawling up the wall. Right then I jump up, lift Zaharin Smyadovski, and dump the soldier onto the sergeant's head. I hear the two of them tumble down in a shapeless ball, swearing at me like even a sailor wouldn't.

I look around and find myself standing on the corner of Pirotska Street and the canal, by the local playground. I cross the tracks of streetcar Line #3 and see on the corner to the left a newly-built puppet theater, bursting with the joyful noise of Young Pioneers.

16

The cold cut right through my waist, but my soul filled with hope as I saw a streetcar approaching. It rumbled past me along the tracks and drew to a halt at the stop. Future generations, brandishing red neckerchiefs, got on by command, and the streetcar rang out lovingly and began to go on. Almost out of breath, I lunge forward with clattering shoes, bushes lash me across the face, walls jostle me, the sidewalk is tripping me, until finally my palms stick to two ice-cold brass handles and I leap into the last carriage amid a swarm of kids, right at the moment when the streetcar is smoothly picking up speed.

I make my way forward, pinching flushed cheeks, whistling a tune so as to dispel my young companions' surprise, and reach the front door. I stick my head outside to make sure nobody is chasing me, and lo and behold—I *am* being chased! Lomski and Smyadovski in single file are catching up with the streetcar and are just about to get on. Right then, I remember an old neighborhood trick from the game Hare and Hounds along the route of Line #3. I jump off and dart toward the sidewalk. The two uniforms have just boarded but now drop back to the pavement and dart after me while the streetcar is visibly breaking away from us. I keep running along the sidewalk, and they gradually catch up until suddenly, in utmost exertion, I rush forward, catch the streetcar, pull myself up by the handles, and set one foot on the step of the last carriage while my other leg is dangling somewhere on the side.

My pursuers try to do the same. The soldier, being more agile and dodgy, had already grabbed on with one hand when I turned around, rammed his cap all the way down to his nose, and undid his fingers from the brass. Then he really grew ferocious, but he lost his balance, plumped down on his stomach, and started bouncing along the pavement from the force of the momentum, until his body got tangled in the legs of the sergeant running behind him, who in turn tripped over and met the pavement with his forehead.

I was out of danger, at least for the moment. I sat down on the carriage step and began to regain control of my lungs, which were agonizing from lack of oxygen.

The streetcar stopped at Bregalnitsa Street. I jumped to the pavement and glanced up toward Nishka Street. I felt a sudden urge to head toward home and my heart sank, but I showed a strong will and broke into a run in the opposite direction down toward Slivnitsa Boulevard, aiming to take the canal to the Lions Bridge, and from there, according to the plan, on to the Orlandovsti cemetery.

I felt like I had sunk into weightlessness, as if I'd come from a different planet and I wasn't used to walking on earth. At one point I stopped running and began dragging along. Down the street, everything got deserted, chilly, downright cavernous. The windows and the street lamps emitted a waxy glimmer. I passed the school, my school, the yard, the bench on which I saw her for the first time, the janitor's shed. Someone had stepped out for a smoke. Then I see the matchbox factory, the bakery, and next to it the house in which Gosheto once lived—he was a real good egg, only he fell from the roof of the chocolate factory with a bag of lemon-slice candy and killed himself. Then out of the darkness up sprung the silhouette of the balcony where one morning we saw his father hanging by his neck. I stop at the corner of Bregalnitsa and Tsar Simeon and see in front of me a community center and behind it a polyclinic. Something starts to click in my head, and here I am heading that way without much hesitation.

17

I approach the polyclinic entrance stealthily. I look around—everything is deserted, not a living soul in sight. I raise my arm hesitantly and ring the bell, my finger icy, about to break. I wait. Some time goes by and nothing happens. Then from somewhere within, a woman's tobacco-stained voice wafts my way, talking to me as if it sees me, while I see no one.

"Hey, you . . . yes, you, with the suit, come on in!"

I pull myself together and creep into an empty hallway. I hear steps echoing, the scraping of leather soles and shoe tacks on the cement. I gaze at photographs on the wall, scenes of athletic parades, cross-sections of internal organs, and diagrams tracing infectious processes.

The Wired Radio Outlet was recapping news headlines, then gave temperature readings, and closed with Exact Time. The time was 20:35 when I turned along the hallway and saw at the far end an open door. I entered timidly. Inside a female doctor fixed me with a rusty stare, rollers in her hair, large glasses, a white uniform, tight in the waist, and brand new ankle-boots.

"Comrade, are you drunk by any chance? You have a poisoned look. And what is this shabby suit with a hole in the shoulder and dirty wadding sprouting out of it . . . Are you from the circus or something?"

"No," I say, confused, but suddenly something pops into my head and I add, "The suit is from the theater company . . ."

She shakes her head "no" and rollers rattle.

"No, no, it's true," I say. "We're rehearsing *Under the Yoke* back there at the community center, I play Boycho Ognyanov, an intellectual *à la mode*, but I'm wounded . . ."

"Ognyanov, I'm just about ready to believe you."

"No, see . . . it's the dramatic treatment, really daring and unusual."

I thought of the Boycho Ognyanov bluff completely out of the blue, but just in time, as if an invisible prompter had provided it to save me from humiliation and unmasking. I had completely forgotten about the hole, from the bullet Slug plugged me with. I looked, and indeed the hole was still there, only it was now larger and definitely more frayed.

"Stop kidding . . . Your eyes say otherwise!" She doubted my words and peered into my eyes, her gaze scratching, as if manicured.

"No, I'm serious," I insist on my story. "While rehearsing on stage I felt sick. I had some mushrooms and now I'm nauseated, my legs are failing me, my eyes are burning."

"Ognyanov, this story of yours sounds lame. We'll need to run some tests."

The doctor turned backward sharply, and her neck, dry and sinewy, got twisted like ship's rope. Then her sinews shortened and she yelled:

"Nurse, drain Ognyanov . . . run blood . . . and urine, so we can see what brings this amateur actor here!" Then she looks at me with her gaping eyes, winks, and adds, "Are you skipping out or something? Need a sick note to leave the theater troupe and escape from 'under the yoke'?" and she starts giggling, a tobacco phlegm rippling in her throat.

Responding to the call, from a door inside the office came a large-boned woman, looking as if she had been stuffed into her white uniform, her hair braided into what looked like a large sticky bun, and with a visibly enlarged windpipe. First she eyeballed me from beneath a greasy bang, then she came close, wedged herself tightly against me, and uttered directly into my nose in a tart barrel breath:

"Come with me to the lab and roll up your sleeve."

The nurse did an about face as if by command, struck a heel on the floor, and trundled along. I followed her silently.

The Wired Radio Outlet infused the lab with Viennese waltzes. This seemed to soften the nurse's polyclinic temper, and she shook her hips foxily. She seated me on a swivel chair and said:

"Do you have a file with us?"

"I don't think so."

"What do you mean *think*?"

"I'm new to the neighborhood. Before that I was a tinsmith in Banishora, and now I'm apprentice designer in the packaging department at the chocolate factory."

"Malchika?"

"Yes, and this is my first visit here."

"First and last name, address, age, education level, marital status." The nurse was sitting ready to fill out some document titled "People's Republic of Bulgaria" and below that, "Medical File."

"Christophor Javacheff, 5 Tri Ushi Street, age thirty-three, elementary education, spinster."

"I'm a spinster, you're a bachelor . . . Elementary education, clearly, but the age is Christ-like . . . Hold on a minute . . . Tri Ushi is in another district, what are you doing here?"

"Like I already said, I'm performing in the community center theater company, and I felt a stab in the stomach, a terrible one!"

"You're rehearsing very late . . . on an empty stomach!" Then she started to giggle somewhat theatrically, but it was only afterward that I realized she was kind of hitting on me.

She tied a worn-out piece of rubber around my arm and began to draw blood with sweaty fingers, while her mouth is watering and she starts squirting saliva through her teeth. I look up at one corner of the ceiling. It was all bloated, bulging, hanging, about to fall. A giant, yellowish stain loomed around a thick pipe with a big ring, which oozed treacly, slimy moisture.

"You got some thick vein, comrade!"

She pocketed the vial containing my blood, gave me a cup, and told me to go into the bathroom upstairs and urinate.

"Do you see this pipe, that's where the patients' toilet is," as she pointed upward with a practiced gesture, her uniform lightly sliding up her thigh and baring the clip of a reseda garter. "You urinate in the cup. You'll see instructions there how it's done."

"Will do!"

I headed to the bathroom, wondering what I was going to learn about myself.

"You're in luck," the nurse says later as she picks up the cup filled with warm piss. "The lab technician agreed to run your tests this evening . . . A really, really well-bred man . . . and to tell you the truth . . . a box of liquor-filled chocolates from you wouldn't do him one bit of harm!" She winked at me and asked me to wait for the results in the hallway.

"We'll call you when they're ready." She set off, then came back and whispered, "Should I give you a bucket if you're still nauseated?"

"No, just my eyes are burning."

"Bite the bullet."

"What bullet?"

"Figuratively speaking."

"OK."

I was left in the hallway, all alone with that phrase, "bite the bullet." My vision had become really painfully intense. I suddenly hear heavy footsteps from the street and prick up my ears, and then someone's tin voice screeched the absurd line:

"And the geography classroom pointer—straight in the ears!"

The entrance door slammed, and someone came into the polyclinic. Then the hallway resounded with a theatrical voice enunciating a rather strange, almost cryptically incoherent word, shifting the stress:

"Labardan . . . la-bar-daaan . . . Labardan-din-don . . ."

Two young men who looked to be students appeared, red caps thrust in their trouser pockets, white nylon shirts unbuttoned at the chest under black jackets, one of them scrawny and practically hauling the other one on his shoulder. As they shuffled their feet, the shoe leather swishing on the cement drove me insane.

"Vladislav, sit down and behave yourself because I'll waste you, man!"

The scrawny one shot these words into Vladislav's face and unloaded him onto the bench right next to me. Meanwhile, Vladislav was tuning up his voice.

"You . . . yes, you, the patient in the gabardine, where is the X-ray room?" He looked at me with a bloodshot eye. "'Cause Jitterbug here jumped out of the third floor and smashed his ribs."

"Was he caught doing someone's wife?"

"Not at all," he answers. "He was soused, and in the whirlwind of the dance he did a somersault, flew out the balcony, and shattered on the pavement."

The nurse, who had detected the presence of new patients, appeared visibly refreshed and tidied up, if I may put it that way, and politely asked the two to observe the rules and keep quiet, adding:

"This is internal diseases. X-ray is up the stairs and to your right. The radiologist will take you as soon as he comes back from the cafeteria. He just went to get some soup; we have a long icy night ahead of us."

"The twenty-first of December, the longest night of the year!" I threw in to back up the nurse.

"The longest broth, the greasiest galantine, ga-lan-tine, tin-tin-tin, give me whiskey and gin," Jitterbug started to hum, lapsing into a state of malicious excitement. But right then Scrawny put a hand over his mouth, pierced him with a glare, and held him that way until he drifted off.

Silence reigned.

At one point I heard someone entering the polyclinic, and in a moment a man stood in the doorway—well built, cotton in his ears, bandaged with gauze—and started explaining somewhat flustered:

"Just need the bandages changed . . ."

We must have been staring at him in ridicule, because he reacted with pronounced testiness:

"What's wrong?"

"Nothing . . . just wondering how you burned your ears?" I ask curiously.

"O-h-h-h," says he, "louder 'cause I can't hear . . . can't you see I got cotton in my ears!"

"How did you burn yourself?" I raise my voice.

"Simple! I'm having a beer and listening on the Wired Radio Outlet to the national soccer finals— Levski v. CSKA—and my wife is ironing bed sheets . . ."

He sat at the end of the bench and started to slide toward us.

"Then what?" says Scrawny.

"Huh?"

"Then what?"

"Oh . . . nothing," the man with burnt ears shrugs his shoulders. "When Levski scored their first goal, the phone rang, and in my state of extreme excitement, I picked up the iron instead of the phone, stuck it to my ear and missed the call."

"OK," ponders the student, "but why both ears?"

"Huh?"

"Why both?" Scrawny screams.

"Well, when Levski kicked a second goal, the phone rang again," said the man with burnt ears. Then he stared at the floor and grew sad.

"Not to worry!" Scrawny comforts him. "You got away easy, could have been much worse. The latest issue of *Amateur Arts* tells about a certain mower, writer, and accordionist. He's coming home one evening from the fields, scythe over his shoulder, thinking about the nature of conflict-free dramaturgy and the accordion's role in it. Suddenly an ugly toad flops down at his feet. He reaches to slash it with the scythe but instead chops off his head."

"Nothing new under the sun!" Jitterbug concludes in a daze. "The law of universal iniquity had already been noted in ancient times when Archimedes determined experimentally that any given slice of bread always falls on the buttered side."

An uneasy quiet set in.

"Ah," Scrawny calls out, "did you hear what happened to the prima donna of the National Theater, Stomna Gulabova?"

"Gulabova who?" asks the man with burnt ears.

"Stomna!" shouts the student.

"Oh, the bosomy one who played the agronomist in the *Old Timers* trilogy?"

"Yes, that one."

"So what about her?"

"Well, last weekend she goes skiing in the Rila Mountains. She's climbing up the slope sideways on her skis, but then she feels the urge to piss. She sneaks into some bushes off to the side, pulls down her ski pants, and still on her skis she squats and starts relieving herself. But suddenly she loses her balance, the skis take off down the slope, and Stomna finds herself flying down the middle of the ski run with her panties off."

"Then what?"

"Then what?"

"Then what?"

"Nothing. When she sees she's nearing the lodge at the bottom of the hill, she squats again, undoes her Kandahar cable bindings, and plunges sideways into the snowdrifts. She breaks an ankle but manages to save face by pulling up her pants before the ski patrol arrives. They take her to the hospital in Samokov, her leg is set in a cast, and they begin filling out her paperwork. Meanwhile an ambulance brings in an unconscious mountaineer with a cracked head, and Stomna finds out that the poor fellow fell off the ski lift as he leaned out to follow with his eyes a renowned actress with a bare ass flying down the run in breakneck slalom."

The man with the burnt ears clicked his tongue and said to Scrawny, "A trumped up affair. That story is quite lame . . . a national prima donna skiing bare-assed . . . yeah, right, and I was born yesterday. Cruel fate lashes out elsewhere—in the neighborhoods, among us, the rough, ordinary, simple folk, where every single life constitutes a bouquet of harsh slaps in the face!" The man with burnt ears pounds himself in the chest and keeps cogitating in a loud voice, "Because iniquity is universal for some but not for others. Just last summer, for example, friends came to borrow my motorcycle with the sidecar, because I'm the only person in the neighborhood who has one . . ." He grew quiet here, looked at us, and then asked:

"Guys, am I shouting too much?"

"Yes."

"Huh?"

"Yes!"

"Aha, that's because I can't hear well . . . 'cause they stuffed these cotton balls in my ears . . ."

"That's fine. Go on, talk."

"Right, so Badjo, who lives across the street from me, bought a 'Balkan' moped and mounts it to try it out in the yard, but the front wheel locks, the bike does a front flip, Badjo flies out and crashes right into the windows of the summer kitchen. He got slashed all over, and an ambulance took him straight to the Pirogov E.R. to get him stitched up. Meanwhile his wife uses newspapers to soak up the gasoline that spilled on the tiles, rolls them up into a ball, and throws them into the outhouse. Badjo comes home all stitches and bandages, has a glass of *rakiya** in the open air, loosens up a bit, goes to take a dump, lights a cigarette, and the crapper blows up. The detonation launches Badjo, toilet and all, through the outhouse roof . . . he lands in the garbage dump. So just like that, all scorched and shattered, doubled up and stuck in the toilet bowl, we wedge him in the sidecar of my motorcycle and head straight back to Pirogov."

The voice of the man with burnt ears came to a climax at the word "Pirogov" and suddenly ceased, as if torn. All was silence.

"How absurd!" I exclaim with some delay.

* *Rakiya* is grape or plum brandy.

"Astonishing!" the man with burnt ears wrinkles his forehead.

"Astonishment is an effort to see through the absurd," Jitterbug philosophizes, "to mentally absorb the chaos!"

Silence.

"Huh?"

"Through the dark bosom of Chaos."*

"Dante's *Inferno*, Canto I," Jitterbug informs us.

"A finely formulated idea," the man with burnt ears says ironically. "Maybe I'll burn it in a wood spoon and give it to my wife as a present for Women's Day."

Silence again.

"Just make sure it doesn't go like in Lom."

"Lom?"

"Yes, Lom!" says Jitterbug emphatically and turns to Scrawny: "Lay it on them, Emko!"

"So even there things happen!"

"Some things at that!" Scrawny wrinkles his forehead.

"Such as?"

"Last year on Women's Day, a black cat starts to cross the road, and right across from it a truck is speeding up, full to the top with steel plates. The driver sees the cat, revs up the vehicle, manages to avoid it, and at

---

*The line is from Konstantin Velichkov's late-nineteenth-century Bulgarian translation of *The Divine Comedy*. It is an embellishment not found in the original.

83

full speed enters the intersection. But right then a kindergarten is walking across. The driver slams on the brakes, a steel plate flies out of the truck, smashes the shop window of a hairstyling salon located on the opposite corner, and chops off a whole row of backcombed heads. When he sees that, the driver is seized with horror and drops dead on the spot."

"Poor things, just on the holiday of the comrade-woman-mother."

"Imagine, a group of female *udarniks** decided to get coiffured for the Women's Day banquet at the weaving-mill cafeteria."

Silence.

"We bring on ourselves that which we try to avoid!" Scrawny concludes.

"So you're a real smartass then, huh!" the man with burnt ears attacks Scrawny. "Tell me then, what's two stakes, a rope, a saw, and a hammer . . . huh? What is it? . . . Come on, take a guess!"

The students are silent, and I decide to inquire, so the man with burnt ears doesn't feel snubbed.

"So what is it?"

He keeps quiet for a few moments and then snaps:

"A Siberian toilet."

"What, what," cries Jitterbug. "I hadn't heard that one."

---

*Literally "shock workers"—a Russian term coined in the early years of the Soviet Union to denote an over-productive, zealous worker.

"How is it used?" I ask.

"Very simple. You drive one stake in the snow and tie yourself to it with the rope so the wind doesn't blow you away. You use the other stake to shoo away the wolves that come to bite your ass off. After you thrust out, you use the saw to cut off the frozen shit. That's it."

"And the hammer?"

Right then the nurse shouted from somewhere inside and summoned the man with burnt ears to come in so she could change his bandages.

"You use it to pound back in what's left," he replies over his shoulder, heading toward the lab.

"The guy with burnt ears is for Orthopedics," says Jitterbug with a slur.

"How do you figure?"

"His stories are so lame."

"All stories are lame!" Scrawny concludes "If it isn't lame, a story is nothing more than a case of natural science . . . 'cause the amazing part lies in the way it's put together, right, Emko?"

"Precisely!" Scrawny confirms, "just like in the story with the Leica."

"Precisely!" Jitterbug mutters.

The student body fell silent. The stillness weighed down on me, and I broke it.

"What story is that?"

"This story is passed from class to class at the Institute, an old story dating all the way back to the years of Stalin's personality cult."

"So what is it?"

"A seemingly normal one. Two students get married and for their honeymoon they take a trip with a group of vacationers, a group composed of equal parts workers and intelligentsia for the purpose of class amalgamation. Among them are suntanned female teachers from a night vocational school, women of middle and advanced age who've conquered peaks and valleys, with edelweiss in their hair, carrying worn haversacks stuffed with crumpled newspapers in case of an urgent "call of nature." The vacation is in full swing. The newlyweds, who have a Leica camera, pose in front of it madly in love, snapping themselves and the relaxation of the working class. In the group there is a sorehead lathe operator, who tells them, 'I shit on your Leica!'"

Scrawny paused and yawned.

"Then what?"

"Nothing. The days go by and the vacation is coming to a close. The last night the group, properly class-amalgamated, is roasting mussels on a tin plate, drinking, and singing camp songs. At daybreak, the newlyweds return to their bungalow and find it broken into, but luckily nothing is missing, not even the camera."

"Wow!"

"Odd, right? Think again. When they get back home, they develop the film and the answer appears in front of their eyes. One of the snapshots is a close-up of the turner's ass, with toothbrushes sticking out of it! . . . Get it?"

"Toothbrushes?"

"Yes, theirs!"

"How many toothbrushes?"

"Two . . . I don't know, however many they had brought."

"Then what?"

"Nothing. When they see this, they realize that during the vacation a silent class war had been waged against them."

"OK, but what's so lame about this story?"

"What do you mean *what*! Think for a second . . . How do you figure the turner would be able to take a picture of himself in such a pose?"

"Here's how!" Jitterbug grew animated, stood on his feet, and then twisted over in an effort to demonstrate the possibility in question, but a pain stabbed him in the ribs and he sprawled back on the bench.

Stillness engulfed the building yet again. Suddenly the tobacco-stained voice sliced through the silence with an authoritarian falsetto:

"Javacheff, come in!"

And I went in. It is murky inside. The doctor is pacing back and forth, a test tube in her hand. She strikes a heel on the floor and stares fixedly at the ceiling. Then she lowers her head, darts a knobby eye at me, and her look starts to wander over my face, as if cutting up a corpse with an electric welder.

"Iridium! Ognyanov, do you know what iridium is?"

I am silent and at a loss.

"Poison!" Silence, the strike of a heel on the floor, and again: "An insidious, lethal, luminescent poison . . . a poison for which there is no known antidote."

Her lips turned chalk-white and things grew scary. The operative phrase was "there is no known antidote." Then the doctor snapped her fingers, and the nurse immediately turned off the light, as if expecting the cue all along.

The darkness that conquered the room didn't arrive alone. A devilishly glowing spot in the shape of a severed finger was born in it, some ashen radiation, which started shaking and spelling out in the dark the word *i-r-i-d-i-u-m*. It was the test tube in the doctor's hand.

Her voice resounded and spit out the following opinion regarding my case:

"Hocus pocus and then mortus, lights!"

The lights came on. Silence . . . the strike of the heel on the floor, then the doctor again:

"This luminescent poison was found flowing through your veins . . . in other words, you, Ognyanov, have been poisoned, but not with mushrooms. You are a goner and there is no coming back, but we will fight for you . . . Don't look at me like an imbecile. First we'll report you to the police so that an investigation into the case can begin, and then we'll take you by ambulance to the toxicology department at the Medical Academy. There, they will change your blood. Now think, think carefully, and tell us, do you have any idea or even a theory about when and how exactly you could have ingested this poison?"

I hesitated a moment and then shook my head.

"Then someone else gave it to you."

"For what reason?"

"For a simple reason—to murder you!"

The blood fled from my face. I turned pale.

"A murder has been committed with you . . . You've been murdered, Ognyanov . . . murdered on the spot!"

I stood there crushed, grubbing the floor with my eyes. The operative phrase now was "murdered on the spot." The doctor kept hammering the bare facts into my head.

"Do you realize the severity of the situation you are in? We are talking about an actual murder, and you are the victim, but who is the murderer, huh? Who? . . . Nurse, call the police precinct and tell them that the murdered is alive. Ognyanov, you lie down right away . . . you need an IV."

The operative phrase became "the murdered is alive."

The course of action suggested by the polyclinic was completely unacceptable to me. I glanced at the door and saw the bow of a key in the lock. I reached across the desk where the doctor was sitting. She flinched—scandalized, as if I had tried to grab her by the bra straps—but instead I snatched the telephone and ripped the cord with an abrupt twist. I was doing all that with an unperturbed stone face, as if I had turned into a robot—a circumstance that apparently impressed the medical staff because they were staring at me petrified.

I grabbed the key, opened the door, and left, slamming it behind me. Then I inserted the key on the outside, turned it, and the latch clicked. Right then I heard the nurse charge the door like a bull. She started banging maniacally with head and fists, dug into it, and began swearing in the rhythm of the blows she was delivering in a progressively fading tempo.

The student body was slumbering in the hallway. Jitterbug, sprawled on the bench, groaned heavily in a drunken half-sleep interrupted by bouts of coughing. Scrawny woke up from the banging, got unwholesomely animated, a bluish flame flared up in his eyes, he stuck a scrawny pinkie in his scrawny ears, and hissed in a scrawny voice:

"And the geography classroom pointer—straight in the ears!"

Exact Time announced the hour. It was 21:45. Prince Igor's aria from the eponymous Borodin opera emanated from the Wired Radio Outlet.

18

The moon met me outside, white and tender like a girl's knee trying to peek from under a nebulous skirt. I was done for. I only had enough time left to settle a score or two, to thwart someone's plan before the end arrived.

Suddenly, I don't know why, I happened to remember Van Voorst the Eye and thought to myself that he must be watching me from somewhere in the dark bosom of the cosmos and saying:

"Drop it, Moth, just forget about the whole thing altogether!" and I tell him "OK!" and then I turn around and set off, but not toward where he is pointing, because something inside me is tugging at me and is now towing me in the wrong direction.

Exhausted and all dried up on the inside like a biblical camel amid the endless human desert, I set out along the snowy alleyways toward St. Nicholas of Sofia Church, of which I could catch a diagonal glimpse through crowns of bare branches at the other end of the playground. Some insurmountable weakness was propelling me to the place where I had been baptized. There, on the day before the robbery, Ada and I went to swear our love, and Father Todor became our witness and also our father, because we had no one else. She had asked that we do it—if not in front of the whole world, then at least before a holy man—that I should declare I loved her and would take her to be my wife when it was all over.

The outline of St. Nicholas of Sofia rose in a slow, geological manner from the black earth in front of my eyes as I ran toward it. When I got close, I started looking around stealthily, but then I decided to go all the way around to make certain my pursuers weren't prowling about. When I was sure I was all by myself, I mustered up my courage and ascended the steps leading to the entrance gate.

The heavy gate yielded with difficulty and started to creak as befitted an ancient sanctuary. I make my way inside, where everything is dying out—not just vigil lights and candles—everything is slowly wasting away: the iron, the plaster, the stained glass.

Misery, decay, and a hollow echo. The sexton— demonically scraggy, as if dropped out of a Brothers Grimm tale, his posture crooked like a candelabra forged by some evil, bungling genius. He was putting out candles with bony fingers and mumbling something to himself. A smoky ribbon of incense twisted into the air, slowly merged with my breath, and neutralized the evil holed up inside me.

Incense heals the distressed soul, embalms it, and thus makes it live for ages.

I take a timid step forward and notice the big icon of the Virgin Mary with the Christ Child. I recognize it immediately: my grandfather Sando used to pray in front of it, while I would look at him and wonder what was going through his mind at that moment of utmost spiritual reclusion. I approach in order to pray as if I were him, but what awaited me there abruptly disturbed my inner peace.

A bill was sticking out of the icon, folded in four and tucked tight into the frame, and the amount—the amount was good. I know I sinned, but something inside me pushed my arm, and I stoop as if to pray, pinch the dough with two fingers, and slip it into the side pocket of my gabardine. I was ready to mumble some prayer, to get up and leave the scene of transgression, but suddenly the silence gave birth to a voice—a withering voice that came with the sound of slow steps and labored asthmatic breathing. It said:

"Before quitting this place, a person does not take without leaving, just like the soul takes its due from this world, but leaves the body as pawn for that which it has taken."

I froze on the spot and my face sagged in shame. I knew the voice full well—the voice of Father Todor. I turned and looked at him from the bottom of my soul.

"Father, I came to leave . . . but the devil stuck a crooked finger into my brain and my hand reached out . . ."

I was about to return the bill, but the priest raised his hand high in the air and pronounced:

"What has been taken remains taken!"

In the absurd situation in which I found myself, I anxiously thrust my hand into the gabardine, took out my own relics—the artificial eye, the letter, the post-card—and said:

"Here, Father, I leave what is most precious to me . . . My hand reached for another's possessions, so that it can leave its own in return."

He came close and spoke straight into my face:

"You have fallen as low as a worm, son . . . you've died out! . . . There is no more wick left in you, just a lump of wax suggesting that at one time something deep inside there used to burn . . . Lev, what path did you take to lose yourself so?"

He said my name and thus crushed me completely, as if my soul staved in and I caught sight of the end.

"You recognized me, Father . . . you recognized me!" I said choking and collapsed all shattered at his feet, while he laid his heavy palm on my head and said:

"Lev, how could I not recognize you! It was this very hand that baptized you!"

I burst into sobs. My insides were about to rend apart.

"Why did you come?"

"To repent before I depart forever, Father."

"We will all depart someday. Whence do you come and where are you headed?"

"I was set free today, but I did not find freedom . . . I am on my way to my senseless death . . . A few hours ago I found out I've been poisoned . . . Evil remembers, Father . . . it schemes against me, creeps after me, until it destroys me."

"You speak unintelligibly, your mind is rambling, as if harboring something awful inside itself. Something is tormenting you . . . speak up so your heart lightens. Name your sin."

"I have no sins but one, which everyone knows. I served time for it, and while in prison I didn't commit others. I've been expiating it these twenty years. This sin will be the end of me, and it is not my sin only. I chose to take it on myself without anyone having forced me . . . I swear I am not a murderer . . . the murderer is someone else . . . but they caught me, and I chose to keep silent."

"Why . . . who tied your tongue?"

"No one . . . I was silent for her, Father, because she . . . because they only caught me, and she was pregnant, and because of Leo, my son . . . you must have heard about him . . . Do you remember her, Father?"

I gasped for air and my voice died abruptly. Then the priest spoke:

"I remember . . . and people remember . . . they gossip . . . ask questions . . . a boy and a girl . . . two dewdrops . . . and then mud . . . A rumor spread that she put you up to it . . . They put you away, she disappeared, and another rumor spread . . . that she became a dancer in casinos and taverns . . . Then the new regime came, and it turned out that she was living out of wedlock with some commissars . . . there was talk about this other one . . . a slimy type . . . then he also disappeared, and a rumor spread that he was a shady character, but then all of a sudden he came down from the woods with the Partisans, put on an epaulet, and became a big shot . . . All sorts of rumors floated around, but what was right and wrong in them there was no one to say."

I raised my eyes humbly and saw the priest's face hanging heftily over me, as if infused with asphalt, detached from the world around us, thrust into the enormous somber dome. I shook off that image and started blathering.

"I have no time left, Father . . . hours . . . I was released from prison today and am being chased again . . . I was hoping that I'd find the right path . . . but I'm not running along it now, Father!"

"You say you are about to depart . . . Which path exactly do you wish to take, what will you lean on, and where will you find strength to walk this path and to retrieve what you have lost, not what is precious, but what is priceless . . . that which defeats the end?"

"The day of reckoning has come. It's time to pull out the slate. Tonight I will figure the final balance, before I am gone forever."

"You will figure the balance . . . How, if your soul is troubled? . . . your mind is entirely in the dark . . . you will judge without knowing the truth . . . you are delirious."

"No! I may be wrong, but I am not in the least delirious . . . This is the only woman I've known, because I loved her . . . The truth is there, Father, in her."

"You, child, are a place where something divine has transpired, something that doesn't belong to you, something that you have no right to judge . . . you have no access to it either with your will or your mind . . . the thing called life, the unattainable, the enigma . . ."

"I atoned without having sinned!" I cut short his tirade. "I leave here these personal belongings for your safekeeping, Father Todor, and when you hear that I am no more, make sure that these things lie in the earth along with me . . . The place should bear no sign of a grave . . . Thorns, Father, bare thorns!"

I started to shiver. He takes the items from me with one hand and with the other pats me on the head and says:

"Be humble, son . . . you are feverish, be humble."

"I beg you, Father, with my whole decrepit soul I beg you, do me this final kindness!"

An oppressive silence set in, and then his voice resounded suddenly with deliberate force:

"Either you don't know what you're saying, or I don't know how to understand it." He began coughing anemically, and when he was quiet his speech returned: "You need to realize, son, that whatever you do, you won't get to the truth. Your truth is not her truth. This woeful tale has another ending too—for you to stay here, with me."

He pulled me up by the shoulders, and I stood up with a sharp pain in my legs. He looked at me worried and his voice grew firm:

"Choose, son, the monastery or the world!"

"The world, because I have scores to settle with it. Bless me, Father, because I will expire in carnal passions, not in a monk's calm."

"May God be with you, Lev!" He made the sign of the cross over me and then said: "Wait here! I will bring you something warm to put on. You are all blue from the cold."

He disappeared in the darkness of the church and in a short while reemerged with a coat in hand. He threw it over me, kissed me on the forehead, and sent me away with the word:

"Live!"

At the threshold, before slamming the gate behind me, I stopped, turned back, and saw on the cavernous church vaults how a shadow hunched with arthritis was stepping from leg to leg, hiding its face in enormous palms.

19

Death and the internal organs of the state were at my heels. I was striding fast, but not too fast, so I wouldn't draw suspicion. I found an old beret in the pocket of the coat Father Todor had given me, and clad in it I felt considerably better in terms of both the cold and my fear of being identified. There was something else, though, in the other pocket, which I felt only now. I reached in and froze—my hand felt the three items I had left with him for safekeeping. The old man hadn't believed me. My story must have sounded lame. He had sent me off to live, not die. Everything I owned I was now carrying on me.

A blackness, cloying like molasses, issued along Nishka Street, broken up in places by a demonically ephemeral light sprinkled from the street lamps like lunar dust. At the end of the street, more light flared up, but of a completely different, monumental nature. I felt I was walking through a tunnel leading to some unearthly sunspot.

I reached The Grey Horse tavern and almost by reflex peeped through the frosted window, and what do I see—everything inside is just like in the old days, as if I had been pulled far back in time. The neighborhood kibitzers, seated around the tables in twisted poses, were drinking shots of *rakiya*, nibbling on pickled cabbage with paprika, and heatedly wrangling over something.

I make up my mind and walk in to sniff the past, and as I walk in, a reddish fellow with a tilted cap waves at me and says, "Hey, pal, come over here a second!"

I hesitantly approach the table where the person in question is seated together with two similar characters wearing rubber loafers, smeary quilted work jackets, and dingy dungarees, their noses fleshy and porous, as if larded. They are drinking some brownish sludge with lemon slices.

"Sit down," says the kibitzer, "'cause I got something to ask you."

"How come you decided to ask me?" I wonder and take a seat at their table while pulling the coat off my shoulders because I was hot.

"'Cause you're young," says this person. "You look like you completed at least eighth grade. But now that I see your gabardine, I'm thinking that you even went to high school, right?"

"Yes, the one that burnt down." I'm pulling his leg.

"Come on now, I'm good at sizing up education levels."

"OK, go ahead, ask!"

"Here's the thing," he drags on the dying cigarette butt and puts it out in the albata ashtray. "We are gathered here, all simple folk, drunks—myself, a warehouse-man; this guy here, a tinsmith, we call him Gosho the Tinhead; and this one is the carpenter, Pesho the Jigsaw. He's been knocking himself out all these years and still can't manage to finish vocational night school. Anyway, we've been drinking this here stinking guck with a tinge of stinkhorn—it's called 'rum'—and we've been puzzling how that song came about, the one about the fifteen men in the dead man's chest, yo-ho-ho and a bottle of rum. What's the deal anyway, 'cause it's kind of pointless, it's sort of lame . . . if you catch my drift. Who are these fifteen men and what the heck are they doing in some dead man's chest, all together with a bottle of rum? Let's see if you can decipher the image!"

I look at him and think to myself, "Sure I can decipher it, 'cause I graduated from the University of Van Voorst the Eye," and I say with a melancholy smile:

"This story was created beyond the ocean, in olden times. The settlers in the American colonies who wanted to be buried in their homeland were transported across the ocean once they died, submerged in brine, and the more affluent—in rum barrels. The pirates would attack these ships because of the rum, part of which they would drink themselves, while the rest got sold in ports around the world. The song talks about fifteen drunken pirates who fell inside such a coffin full of rum, and yo-ho-ho is the equivalent of our ha-ha-ha."

"Waiter!" yelled the kibitzer, "a shot of rum for the young fellow, right away, 'cause he opened our eyes."

"You can't beat erudition," says the Tinhead.

The waiter, with a golden tooth, a tallowed fore-lock, and a grimy apron, places a shot of rum in front of me. I raise glasses with the kibitzers and down them.

"Who are you?" asks the one who called me over.

"Christophor. And you?"

"They call me Il Patiento."

"Why?" I ask, puzzled, and the Jigsaw starts to explain, "Listen, buddy, let me tell you what this dork here did to earn his nickname."

The Jigsaw sipped from the next newly-served rum and began his story:

"So, this guy right here is lining up at lunch time at the cash register of the cafeteria on Slaveykov Square to pay for his stuffed grape leaves. He's waiting quietly for his turn, with this same cap on his head. Then the cashier notices that a trickle of blood is streaming down his temple, and this guy here, staring at the ass of the woman in front of him, suspects nothing. The cashier gets scared, and while he's still sitting at his register, quietly so he doesn't cause undue panic, picks up the phone and calls emergency. The ambulance arrives right away. The paramedics see that fresh blood is streaming down the side of our man, and without much dallying they grab him, take away his grape leaves, sprawl him on the stretcher, put an oxygen mask over his mouth, stick him in the ambulance—and straight to Pirogov. There they start unpacking him, finally take off his cap, and lo and behold—sitting on his bald pate is a raw pork chop, freshly seasoned with onions, pepper, and parsley. The smartass wanted to take it without paying!"

"Then what?"

"Nothing!" says Il Patiento. "I didn't notice the blood 'cause I thought I was sweating. It was pretty darn hot. They took away the pork chop, told me to go to hell, and kicked me out with the words 'you're a patient for the slaughterhouse.'"

The others started giggling, but Il Patiento countered:

"The Jigsaw here knows to tell tall tales about other people, but he's all mum about himself . . . about that embarrassment on his name day."

"Embarrassment?"

"Hell, yes. 'Cause see, the Jigsaw treats himself that day right here at the tavern to baked beans, cabbage, and beer, and then goes home, while the wife had a surprise in store for him. She grabs him at the door, blindfolds him, takes him to the living room and seats him at the table. There's a knock at the door, she goes to get it, and lingers there awhile. The Jigsaw, all leavened on the inside, bulging and about to explode, sits blindfolded, awaiting the surprise. The gasses inside him are boiling like hell and demanding a way out. He shifts his weight to his left flank, detaches from the chair, and issues a robust ripple of gasses. To dispel the odor, he grabs the end of the tablecloth and starts fanning with it. He relaxes, but bulges up again, and the exercise repeats itself, then again and again, until finally his wife returns, removes the blindfold, and the surprise flashes before his eyes. Seated around the table were all the guests his wife had secretly invited. They raise glasses to toast the name-day boy, and then—laughter and embarrassment aplenty."

The Jigsaw waves his hand and says to me:

"Don't listen to him, it's all cock-and-bull stories cooked up around the drinking table as mere banter. But check this one out, 'cause it was all written up in an official wall-newspaper, duly archived, no bullshit."

The Jigsaw tosses off the next shot, drags on his Udarnik cigarette, and says:

"Il Patiento is building the Hainboaz mountain pass and goes to contribute to nature in some road-side bushes. When he's all done, he wipes himself with hart's tongue fern, turns around, and what does he see— there's no shit. He gets the shivers and thinks to himself, 'an anomaly,' 'cause he'd just learned the word. Then oddly the anomaly is repeated. This guy goes number two again, but still no shit appears. The man gets depressed, feels like crying out his insides. He goes to an esteemed *udarnik* to seek advice, and the guy quizzes him: 'We build the road, and the road builds what?' 'Us!' replied our man. 'Correct!' said the *udarnik* and clued him in on what the deal was. It turned out that because he was a rookie, two smartasses from the crew colluded 'to slip him the shovel,' in other words, they secretly stick it under his ass while he's taking a dump and use it to remove his shit before he turns around. Because, by some unwritten law of natural science, a man in this situation always turns around to take a look."

At that point the Wired Radio Outlet began playing the song "You Are My Mermaid, I Am Your Drowning Sailor," and the whole tavern took up the tune and started grating on my ears.

"This is the one, the song of the Bulgarian pirate!" Il Patiento cried exaltedly, then got up, dragged himself to the Wired Radio Outlet, stood on his toes, and kissed it.

"Listen, buddy, never trust the Wired Radio Outlet when soused!" he tells me after sitting back at the table.

"Why not?" I ask.

"'Cause here's the thing about it," he says gloating. "So that he can sober up before going to work one morning, this here nitwit, the Tinhead, decided to do some exercises as directed by the Wired Radio Outlet. At thirty pushups the speaker tells him, 'raise the right arm.' He raises it, but the speaker must have been a wise guy 'cause then he says, 'raise the left one as well.' The Tinhead follows the command and falls flat on his face on the floor. The imbecile smashed his nose, this here flabby nose," and with two fingers he pinches the said organ.

"Ouuuuuuch . . . you jerk!" squeals the Tinhead and knocks off Il Patiento's cap with a rather uncoordinated swing.

At that point, the tune came to a sudden halt. On the Wired Radio Outlet, Exact Time announced 23:00.

I jumped up double-quick, thanked them for the rum, and dashed out the door fully aware that my time was running out, while they sent me off in one voice, "Be good!"

I continued along Nishka Street at a hurried pace until finally I reached the Vuzrazhdane cinema, where all sorts of people were filing out of the evening show. I stopped in front of the cinema to look at a poster for a film called *The Inspector and the Night*. I admired all these modern people passing by, and only then did I realize how oddly attired I looked in my gabardine.

Next to me at the corner stood a full-cheeked man with an enlarged head, a bowler hat tilted upward, an elephant-skin face, and square glasses with massive lenses like basalt slabs. An incomplete thought resounded in his large nose, which for some reason was fortified on the inside with tampons: ". . . our national cinema rid itself of Stalin's cult . . ."

20

run. Suddenly the street ends, and before my dwindling gaze the center of the capital city unfolds in all its marble-granite might. I find myself drowned in blinding light, as if I were in an ecumenical incubator, in a hatchery with an unearthly design. Overcome by a feeling of blind submission in front of the power of this stone-hewn light, I think to myself, "It has come true!"

The prophetic words of the Wired Radio Outlet in the cooler *had* come true—light had vanquished darkness. I had arrived at the luminescent center of the city, in the throbbing heart of the System, the Communist Party Headquarters. I knew it existed, but I now realized that mere knowledge cannot help you grasp the immediate, mind-boggling appearance of this heart, especially when you are exposed directly to its cosmic pulse, to its ferroconcrete tendons, to its unbreakable cubature, to its stereometric profile, to its cast-iron musculature, to its celestial garrets, to its omnipresent mortar. And on top of the world, the red star glares and darts to the sky like a ruby meteor.

I notice that I'm walking but casting no shadow, and I wonder whether I'm already dead, whether I'm in Kingdom Come, whether I'm at the gates of the Garden of Eden.

Under my feet the ground feels tense, as though pregnant and about to crack.

All of a sudden an eye-vulcanizing sight flares in front of me, and I catch a glimpse of two stalwart sentries standing guard face to face in front of a heavy marble gate, feathers in their heads and flint guns by their feet—troops from the Flying Squadron, now standing like herdsmen, but immobile, as if they were made of tin.*

"The Mausoleum!" I cry in my stomach, and a somber memory rushes into my head, the memory of that ill-fated summer night of 1949 that I spent below ground here, drudging in the foundation pit of this eternal home, the night when Van Voorst the Eye left me forever.

I freeze on the spot and contemplate, goggle-eyed, the Mausoleum—this demonstration of a better life. Due to the violent action of my heart that this causes, I feel elated but refrain from addressing the flying herdsmen.

A moment of full class consciousness arrives, and I decide to dedicate myself to it with all my being. The mummy, I now realize, is the main fuse in that radiant expanse where people bustle about like bits of frag-

---

*The Flying Squadron was a unit organized by Bulgarian revolutionary Georgi Benkovski during the 1876 April Uprising.

ile heating coil. Should that fuse burn out, the expanse goes dark, the heating coils grow cold, and heaven becomes hell.

Foreign words help me figure out the singularity of the moment. "Mummy" comes from the Arabic for *zift*—black bitumen, a powerful resin with embalming properties.

I look at my feet. I'm standing solidly on the yellow paving stones, and their joints are filled with black *zift*. It was almost as though the Leader's mummy had flowed onto the square in order to bind the pavement forever, turning it into an indestructible *terra firma*. It testified to the smelting of the human flesh of a whole nation into a unified and indivisible anointed corpse—a corpse with immortal power.

"And the corpse will rise again, by itself and because of itself, in its carbon totality amid the toiling masses." I chant to myself the Latin maxim learnt from Van Voorst the Eye in order to rhetorically embellish the moment.

I turn around, cross through the square, and passing by the Palace I stand at the top of Malko Turnovo, a steep, narrow, winding alleyway. I start to descend the stairs and suddenly before my eyes looms an electric sign that reads BEERHOUSE-BAR "MOONSHINE." The door is heavy, an exquisite piece, a brass frame inlaid with scenes of a popular, nation-wide ferment, of various types of popular democratic customs, and of agrarian-industrial progress. Red letters on the thick, sooty glass spell "MOONSHINE."

21

I go down the stairs into a murky basement where the muffled rhythm of a double bass reverberates. A clock on the wall shows 23:00 hours, and I think to myself, "This one is slow." In front of me is the gaping checkroom. The attendant, a harsh man with a military haircut, squeezed into a uniform, wearing the telltale shoes of a former serviceman, looks at me as if he can tell who I am.

I ask him who is singing tonight, and he says he doesn't know and can't leave his post to find out. He invites me to go in and check for myself. He reaches for my coat and hands me a tag in return. I take it off but then wave my hand and declare, "It stays with me."

I pay the cover charge with the bill from the church, collect the change, straighten the gabardine in front of the mirror between the two restrooms, and with my heart in my mouth I slowly and somewhat tentatively enter the dining and dancing hall.

Instantly, my eye catches a bright spotlight on a heavy black plush curtain at the far end of the beerhouse.

In front of it a small jazz combo shines like cellophane: a piano, saxophone, double bass, and drums. The musicians, all with military haircuts, shout out in one voice, and somewhat daftly, syllables like "ho-ho-ho" and "boogie, boogie."

A huge globe covered with thousands of pieces of broken mirror turns in the middle of the hall above the dance floor, creating a strange light effect on the walls, ceiling, and floor, something like thousands of shooting stars. The place is intimate and barely half full—actually, nearly empty. The hall is smallish, with a dance floor for a few couples and a dozen tables scattered among the columns around it. Everything in the beerhouse sounds muffled. You could hear a suppressed, by nature slothful and adulterous, carnal nocturne.

To the side of the orchestra spreads a diamond-black bar with large mirrors along the walls and a host of bluish glass bottles lining the shelves. I head in that direction, while in front of me the spotlight glares and whispers, "Look at me."

I sit at the bar where I find perched two odd birds—one, with a drill-bit gaze, stares boringly like a mechanical owl, and the other one sports a bowtie on a bare neck, a silvery cigarette holder, and a forelock that had exploded in the air around him.

The bartender—short, stocky, dark-eyed, and mysteriously dumpy, forged for nightlife—greets me with a bewildered face and a sharply phrased question: "Who let you in?"

"No one stopped me," I start excusing myself. "I was coming down the street, and I decided to drop in and have a drink, listen to some music, like a free citizen in my own country."

"That's fine, but dressed like that . . . the doorman must have taken you for an actor from the Youth Theater—they often stop by straight from the stage, have a shot, and then go change. Who are you?"

"Me?" I stall a bit. "I've come from a festive banquet with my classmates, it's called a retro-shindig, and that's why I put on my father's suit from the old times to spice things up, you know."

"Got it. What are you having?"

"Something strong 'cause I'm feeling down."

"A White Slave."

"White what?" I ask without losing sight of the spotlight.

"The white slave, as a pop song goes, is liquid freshness-ness-ness. The most desirous drink among the artistic intelligentsia."

"Pour . . ."

"Greco. Call me Greco," and he darts an impish look at me.

"Javacheff, Christophor," I introduce myself.

Greco took to shaking vigorously in his hairy arms some sort of metallic thermos, which makes him talk in snatches while the White Slave is roiling inside.

"Who's singing tonight?" I ask while keeping a vigilant eye on the spot with my peripheral vision.

"Gilda, as usual . . . she's taking a break right now . . . then she has one more set and we close."

"Gilda? Gilda, you say?"

"Yes, comrade head-of-personnel . . . I said Gilda. There she is in the photo behind me."

Greco poured a thick, off-white liquid over three ice cubes in a heavy crystal glass and slid it to me down the polished bar. The precious metals on his arms rattled.

I take the White Slave while my glance immediately shoots in the indicated direction, and indeed, there stood a large black-and-white photograph of a woman singing in the spotlight. It was her.

The blood rushed to my head and everything grew loud. I was throbbing on the inside like an infected wound. Right then, the bowtie next to me looked over impishly, then raised a glass and introduced himself Something stirred in his bowels, and they started gurgling like desert reptiles.

"Koko, deputy head of Bulgarian Photo."

"Christophor, designer in the packaging department of the Malchika factory."

"Cheers!"

I raise a glass full of tropical bliss, and I almost splashed it about because my hands were shaking from exhaustion and my lips were burning.

"Yono!" the individual with the drill-bit gaze announces his name. "Yono Dimchev, associate professor and essayist."

Of course I didn't know what line of work an essayist was in, and I didn't give a damn, but in light of the circumstances, I needed to socialize somehow to justify my presence there while awaiting her appearance. Courtesy is foreign to my nature, and after all that had happened to me up to that point, it wasn't easy for me to pull myself together and act like a careless reveler. I gather strength to address the associate professor and essayist, while keeping a steady eye on the spotlight resting quietly on the black curtain:

"Which comes first, the essayist or the professor?"

"An interesting question. Allow me to answer it like this: I'm a professor by day and an essayist come nighttime," Yono smirks and bores about with his eyes.

"How do you square the daily and nightly mental shifts?"

"The humanities make these . . . what did you call them . . . 'shifts' . . . compatible."

"And your subject?"

"Identity."

"No shit!" I exclaimed as though I understood.

"Among friends we call him Identity Yono," Greco interjected sarcastically while mixing up some drink of a toxic color.

I chose to go on with the subject and ask the professor-essayist, "Can you penetrate identity with your mind the same way that a neon beam penetrates an ice cube?"

"Yes!"

"Excellent!" I exclaim and turn toward Koko in an attempt to cover up the nervous tension building up inside me: "A bowtie on a bare neck—a hidden message or what?"

"No, no," Koko cleared his throat, "I lost a bet, and I will be wearing it like this till New Year's."

"A bet?"

"Yes, a bet . . . a moronic one, of course, but a bet nonetheless, and every lost bet needs to be satisfied."

"And who did you make this bet with?"

"With this major, some sort of big gun at the Military Counter-Intelligence. He comes here often because of Gilda, and right here at the bar, while the show is going on, we tend to argue about . . . how should I put it . . . general military matters."

At the sound of the word "major," everything swam before my eyes, and my head started buzzing. I anxiously clinked the ice in my glass and downed the rest of my drink. Then Koko looked at me with a sneer, having obviously noticed my clothes:

"What does this outfit symbolize?"

I sit silent and stare at the spotlight, expecting it to give me a hint with the answer:

"A proverbial drifter," I satisfy his curiosity.

Koko looks at me probingly. The sneer that had taken root in his eyes quickly turns to reprimand and he adds, "You're acting far too idly, my friend, and labor forged us all."

"Manual labor built the human mind!" says Greco.

Something inside me rebelled, some desire to outsmart my interlocutor blinded me for a second, and I said, mustering up all my mental capacity:

"There is this book *Candide* . . . and near its end the following question is posed: What is more human—to gad about the world aimlessly, to get raped by ferocious Bulgarians, to have your ass chopped off by said party, to have your genitalia dried on a stake, and then be set free to safely go about your way—or to sit on your soft ass and tend your seedbed of root crops, the seedbed that stretches all the way to the end of the world? Which is the more natural condition—the choice is yours!"

"You're wrong!" Yono abruptly reminded us of his existence. "There is no choice at all here. The issue isn't either/or because one squats in the seedbed of life only after one's ass has already been chopped off and one's genitalia dried up!"

At that point a blue-eyed man in a tight navy blue suit and a red tie seated himself next to us at the bar. The newcomer fell into a state of borderline bewilderment, having obviously caught Yono's last phrase, but he recovered quickly and ordered a meringue, a citronade, and a cigarette. He articulated the three words with, how should I put it, sort of an instrumental sonority, as though he had a whistling tooth in his mouth. Then, with emphatic slowness, as though emerging from some murky underground cavity, behind his back appeared a gaunt blondish young man with an unbuttoned rain jacket and curls streaming down his protruding forehead. The young man's eyes filled with blood as the blue-eyed man turned around and shot a glance at him. Then the blondish man's mouth uttered agitatedly:

"Who gave you the right?"

We grew quiet. The situation had become extremely awkward. I looked at Koko with searching eyes, and he whispered to me about the blue-eyed one:

"Aslan Gulabov, engineer of the human soul, a producer-director at the National Theater and a noted educator. He recently staged the celebrated trilogy *Old Timers* with unprecedented imaginative creativity. He also happens to be the husband of the prima donna Stomna Gulabova."

"The one who broke her leg skiing?"

"Yes, which is why the play isn't being performed now,"

The young man obviously managed to get under the blue-eyed one's skin, but the latter contained his temper, and his voice started to undulate and whistle edifyingly:

"The man of the theater is a type of dough, comrade student-applicant, a dough, not a profession . . . a bacillus, a yeast, a person of a special ferment, not a profession, a ferment that sprouts inside the prompt box. How many times do you need to be told, comrade student-applicant, that we, the men of the theater, can recognize each other by the way we smell, by the oiling of our hair, even by our ear wax. Let me tell you straight to your face so you understand once and for all, young man, you are not made of that dough, you don't respond to our yeast. In other words, sorry, you're not up to snuff!"

After having whistled with his hollow tooth the last string of sibilants, the engineer of the human soul snapped his fingers and the young man, visibly entranced and somehow internally enlightened, said in a feigned amicable voice, "Bite me, Gulabov!"

After expressing himself thus, he vanished in the dusk because right then the lights faded to black and darkness engulfed the beerhouse. An ornate Turkish curse resounded in the fallen dark, and then all was quiet.

Only the spot remained, gaping like a white world fitted into a black hole—a hole it started swallowing slowly and hungrily. A graphite-black dress spilling down to the floor, bare milky shoulders, the hair falling in red spurts, and her ashen lips whispered, "Put the blame on me . . ."

The song had a choked quality. Her voice howled and drawled like a wailing siren beckoning to the womb. The words engaged in ruthless copulation.

Her voice suddenly stopped, and an instrumental section followed. The spotlight jerked and fell on Greco, then on Koko, then it started roving over the faces around me until it settled on mine.

I froze, blinded . . . Then a muffled woman's cry sounded. A bright light flooded the dining and dancing hall once again, but she was not there. Behind the musicians, the black curtain undulated. I jumped and, before the astounded eyes of my interlocutors, dashed forward, jumping over instruments and people, until I finally disappeared behind said curtain.

I found myself in some sort of backstage room stuffed with props and sets. I began roaming about until I noticed a small hallway leading to the dressing rooms.

I stopped in front of a door marked "GILDA." It was ajar so I barged in without hesitating.

22

I encountered her back—sinewy and white, as though whitewashed. Her hair was different—her own black hair, but short, very short. The wig was lying next to her on the floor like a piece of ripped bloody underwear.

Ada was sitting in front of a three-winged mirror and looking into it at me with misty eyes. I froze. I saw myself and was repulsed. I looked absurd and pathetic, like a character in an inept melodrama, caught, dissected . . .

I hate mirrors. I shave without a mirror. I cannot stand my own reflection; it triggers in me a self-destructive impulse.

"You!"

"I!"

"Free?"

"Released."

"Since when?"

"Today."

"You came."

"I found myself here."

"Still, why?"

"Still?"

"Despite everything."

"Despite what?"

"Despite me."

"Despite myself."

"Despite oneself, one is born and dies. The rest one does according to oneself."

"Words learned in the past, from someone, because of someone . . ."

"Words beget words, let's spare them!"

"How can I spare something I don't have!" I exclaimed.

She had already stood up. She had left the mirror. She had turned her face toward me and was now approaching slowly, kindling my soul with her eyes, until she stuck her face onto mine.

I tasted her breath. She explored my moist nostrils with burning lips, passionately pressed herself against me, and her flesh started to quiver. She dug her mouth into my chin and began chewing on it. Then she slid theatrically to the floor, dragging me down on top of her. She was licking my coarse face and thawing it.

She tore away and stood up, unzipped the long black dress, which slowly fell into her feet, and stepped out of it, leaving it gracefully. Now all she had on was a snow-white slip, garters holding graphite-black socks, and red shoes on thin, high heels.

A lightning thrill of arousal shot through my body. I was about to lunge forward, topple her, and possess her with reckless force, but I reached out a bit timidly and held her from behind by her waist. With an extremely dexterous and practiced twisting of the body she slipped like a snake from my foul grip, emitting a choked guttural wail, as if her womb groaned inside her. She snatched from the hanger a black jersey dress, got it on, put on a white silk blouse and a long free-falling wool coat on top. She took my hand and led me out of the dressing room without uttering a word.

Along the narrow hallway, through the back metal door, and down the steep Malko Turnovo alley, we headed toward Prince Dondukov Boulevard. I stopped suddenly and was about to ask something, but she seemed to read my mind because she turned and said:

"Don't ask before you've seen!"

Then she huddled sleepily against me. Pressed to each other, we walked down Serdika Street. We made a turn at the Central Sofia Turkish Baths. It seemed breathlessly hushed amid balls of fumes rising from the stone basins, which shrouded the row of projecting brass spouts. This is where my flight began. I had traveled full circle, and something final was about to happen.

We crossed the streetcar tracks and headed along Maria Louisa toward the Lions Bridge. A dark foreboding seized my soul, intensifying with every step.

The clock on the Market Hall struck midnight.

23

We stopped in front of Number 35—Vlad Lyolyushkin's home.

"Here."

"The crime scene!"

"Let's go upstairs."

I stood there immobilized and looking at her probingly. Then I shifted my eyes sideways and noticed that
the people's authorities had turned the jewelry store into
a general shop: hardware goods and a pharmacy. In the
front window, along with dry herbs, ointments, and
enema requisites, I saw faucets and pipe wrenches lying
about.

"Don't tense up, follow me, upstairs everything will
become clear . . . Believe me, you're in sure hands."

Those last words sounded ambiguous to me. I
advanced hesitantly, but she took my hand and led me
inside the dark entryway, then up the stairs, my shoulder
rubbing against the flaking plaster. I had submitted to
her gentle powers, with which she had completely sub-
dued me. Something else was also drawing me more and

more inward with a strange traction—the place itself, the lair of sin.

I recognized the door. You could see that the frame had once been broken open. She took out a key and unlocked it. We stepped inside. My legs sank under me and my heart was pushed against my windpipe. Blood rushed into my head, which was about to burst from the pressure. I was trying to mentally shrink myself and disappear completely, so that nothing of what was about to happen would physically harm me.

She was walking backward and leading me by the hand with a stare that had the darkness dissolved in it. Our eyes seemed to take up a life of incest, our palms were glued together, our breaths became a single rapid respiration. We were advancing further and further inside the dark apartment. She gripped my arm as if she were holding the weapon of some imminent madness.

I had grown numb—not by the cold, but out of a fear that the past would gape open and the whole bloody affair would take place all over again. Maybe it was because everything inside looked exactly as I had left it twenty years before, down to the last fleck of dust. It was as though I found myself in a museum of my own nightmare.

She turned around sharply, put a light on, and pointed to the dresser. I looked in that direction, and was astonished to see the cast-iron toys arranged exactly the way they were at the time of the robbery. Behind the cupboard glass stood that same African figurine—the cause of all my troubles. I shivered and shot a puzzled glance at her.

"Why did I bring you here, you ask yourself."

"Because the criminal always returns to the scene of the crime," I said as though I had figured things out. "This is the place where he gets caught. Someone needs to be waiting here to catch me. Or am I the one who will be doing the catching? Who am I?"

"No one is catching anyone. I live here . . . alone!"

"Alone! How come alone—at the crime scene without a criminal?"

I was headed for the door, intending to leave this ominous place, but her voice hardened, which stopped me.

"What happens today follows a script . . . a script written by him. For twenty years now he's been waiting for this day to play out according to his plan. But he's wrong."

This stopped me from leaving. Slug had a plan for us once again, so I stayed to thwart it.

"A trap, then! . . . and both of us are in it," I say viciously.

"Yes, a trap, but not for us. Tonight we'll put an end to this theater of shadows. The time machine has stopped, and the two of us will make it run again, run properly."

"Who does all of this belong to?"

"Him."

"He bought the crime scene?!"

The words scalded, as if frost fell on my soul and it wilted.

"The apartment was nationalized," she explained. "He bought it, and now it's his, together with all its belongings, including the diamond, because he believes the stone is hidden here."

"I was here once but saw no stone!"

"Nobody saw it."

"Has anyone lived here since the robbery?"

"No one except me. Heirs from abroad tried to sell the apartment, but then came 9 September. Like I said, time has stopped here. Even the chalk outline of the body remains intact—look."

She pointed to the place and then started advancing toward it, looking at me with lustful eyes:

"Moth, it's just the two of us on stage. Amid all this sham only we two are real. The rest is a trap . . . Time will start moving again for us only if you desire me the way I desire you, here and now . . . truly . . . like for the first time."

The light went out. Ada was standing inside the outline of the dead Lyolyushkin. Having found itself in the chalk circle of the murder, her body bristled like an animal and froze in a strange, stalking posture, as if it was about to pounce.

I moved forward, shaking on the inside.

At that moment, the wall clock struck midnight. Like the crime scene itself, it was drawing us backward.

Her clothes slid down one piece after the other. A snake seemed to be born out of its old skin and curled at my feet—magnetically naked, pining for someone else's flesh.

Seized by somnambulistic arousal, I mounted her.

Copulation is the opposite of self-preservation. In its most innocuous, human form, copulation is a parody of murder.

Take the praying mantis—what an explosive rapacity is hidden inside this most fragile and tender miniature of the fair sex, this most cold-blooded and monstrously ravenous female creature!

She seems to be praying, but in fact she is preying, wrapping inside her pious posture the temper of a sexually predacious monster. When she is in heat, she becomes devoutly humble until some nearby vagrant male specimen mounts her.

She copulates gracefully, sparingly, and somewhat coyly. She wriggles and keeps a vigilant eye on when the sperm will rise. Shortly before ejaculation occurs, she bites off and swallows the male's head. He is thus freed from his instinct for self-preservation, from his fear of castration vis-à-vis the rutting female. For the insemination to be completed, the inseminator's head must be severed and his body utterly maimed.

The praying mantis is the gentlest guillotine ever created. Her forelegs, which aid her in the beheading, look like homemade bow saws. She annihilates with lightning speed. The act of murder cannot be seen by the naked eye. She has a supersonic ear—the peak of her supernaturalness.

Instinctively, the male approaches copulation like a state of emergency imposed by his sexual drive. Decapitated, he doesn't die at once. No longer in distress, he grows sexually stronger, which stabilizes the intercourse. The genitalia, completely unharnessed and not inhibited by the brain, push the remainder of his body toward all-consuming ejaculation. The brainless male mantis is the most precise and infallible sexual piston ever created.

Having been satiated and fertilized, the female mantis will feed her fetus with the nutrient-rich head of the male, which, after swallowing it, she will digest happily for a long time. The inseminator is thus absorbed thoroughly for the benefit of the semen.

25

It was over.

I emerge slowly and painfully from a state of temporary senselessness. I look around and realize that I am lying lifeless and unclad in Lyolyushkin's chalk outline. The way I found myself sprawled out and illuminated by the seemingly tinned moon, I thought that I was him. I imagined how she had copulated with him as well, back then when she waited on him here, at this very place where he later expired in my arms, these very arms that just a moment ago took the heat of her burning flesh.

A thought began to prick my mind like a wood splinter: Somewhere in infinity, every crime derives from a suppressed copulation. I tried to get the thought out of my head, but it kept gnawing at me and driving me crazy until suddenly a ghostly apparition was born out of the night's hem: Slug glided across the room naked, in boots and a military cap, a whip in one hand and a dripping oil can in the other.

I was losing my mind. I wasn't feeling well, I was nauseated again and I was reminded of myself, of the curse of having been born on this creepy earth, creepy the way a reptile feels to the touch.

I raised my head and looked into the moonlit bluish dusk spreading around me. She was not there. Water was splashing in the bathroom. I stood up and turned on the light. I started to dress—it was cold, and I was getting the shivers. I bit at the chunk of *zift*, started chewing, and paced about nervously. Then I stopped and turned on the radio. Midnight melodies flowed through the room. In a little bit, Exact Time announced 01:00. I looked at the clock—it said twelve-forty.

On the wall across from the cabinet was a dusty bookcase containing all sorts of books. It gave me pleasure and peace of mind to sniff old books, to read their titles, feel their spines, inhale their dust. The smell of a well-bound book cures the ailing soul. I don't know why, but it's a fact already recognized in olden times by the monks who invented the ingredients of the glue used to bind books. Old books breathe, and that's why they smell; their breath is dusty because it's ancient.

My fingers started roaming the shelves and my eyes were chasing after them. I pulled out volumes at random, browsing and sniffing them, until suddenly I notice a book placed upside down, with the letters facing downward. I pull it out and leaf through it. It was a volume of letters from jail by the poet-rebel Venets Tsvetarski, sentenced to death for revolutionary activity. It was

titled *Tenderness and Clamor*, compiled by Bozhura Chepinska, a favorite sweetheart of the poet and a poet herself, published in Vienna in 1925.

I open the volume to the ribbon bookmark, turn on
the desk lamp for added coziness, settle down comfortably in the armchair, and begin to read. And just as I
begin, I am dumbstruck. I am reading and don't believe
my eyes, because what I'm reading was Ada's letter to me
about Leo's death. I reached inside my coat and pulled
out the letter in question. She had copied almost the
whole thing from this book. I flew into a rage, and in my
rage I started swearing.

I kick open the bathroom door, and inside, dreamily, steam curls all around her naked body like a mythical
creature, as though copulating with her. I started reading out loud, declaiming with a lump in my throat the
text from Chepinska's original letter in the volume I was
now holding open in my hand:

"*To my master, or rather brother and dear friend, and
mostly husband, her eternal companion, first and last to
know her heart, who endowed her womb with new life, from
his sister, wife, and above all loving slave:*

"*To Venets from Bozhura.*

"*Recently, my fated love, a person I knew not brought
me good tidings about you, that you are still in the prime of
your youth and are not yielding to the fate that punished us
with a horrible sentence by taking you away from me, the
world, and your son—the son you never saw and are doomed
to never see.*

"I know you are not the one who the court decided you are. I know you chose for it to be this way so that Leo would not be born behind the walls of infamy. I pine for you and for your besmirched youth, but this suffering is a remedy for the unbearable prostration that recently befell me with inhuman, horrid force, and it will thus befall you, mercilessly, now that you are reading these lines."

I grew silent, because she had started reciting together with me, and I decided to let her continue on her own:

"Take from my pain, imbibe from its obsidian tincture, because our son Leo is no longer—he is no longer and will never be again, he is gone . . . smitten by a voracious, preying illness, a visitor with a jaundiced eye took him, the meddling fate robbed us of him.

"We buried him yesterday in the Sofia cemetery. We delivered him to the earth where he will remain for evermore as our precious gift to hideous Death.

"This is an obituary, not a letter, which is why its language is fractured and can only weep.

"Come back, I am waiting for you while weaving a cloth of black dolor, with which I will make your bed. Use your mighty elbows to stave off the fake suitors who besiege me, and lie down next to me. I can no longer become your bride but only the mournful tamer of your fiery flesh, and together, mouth in mouth, let's complete our journey.

"With a bloodless face and an ashen heart . . . I love you with insufferable fierceness,

"Ada"

26

She came up to me wrapped in a white sheet, gave me a somewhat cursory kiss, and then said, "I am sinful!"

She took the volume from my hands, dropped it carelessly on the floor, and then tenderly interlaced her hands behind my head and went on:

"I am sinful before you, Lev . . . sinful that it was not I who wrote this letter, I admit . . . but when I read it, I felt it to be mine, and I read it soon after Leo's death. I was so amazed by the striking coincidence of my find, by the beauty of expression and the depth of feeling, that I thought the significance of my serendipitous discovery was not accidental, and I stole it, in my heart."

Here she looked at her own letter to me, which I still held open, then she reached out moodily with one hand to take it from me, while her other hand kept the bed sheet from sliding down her body.

"You've kept it . . . Give it back to me!"

"You don't get back something you never had."

"I had it before I sent it to you."

"You copied it—copy it again!"

I folded the letter and put it away, hiding it from her sight. Her arm remained suspended in the air, outstretched toward me. She stepped forward and placed it on my shoulder, saying, "I copied it, yes! It fell into my hands by divine will . . . I understood it when I read it . . . understand it yourself!"

I tried to understand, but a different thought raced into my head and split me asunder from inside. I freed myself from her arm, which slid down my shoulder, grazing my skin with her nails. I bristled.

I pulled away from her abruptly and started walking backward, emerging from the fragrances still crawling up her steamy body.

I was thinking aloud:

"I understand something else . . . I understand that you were already living here at the time of Leo's death . . . with our son and with the slug-major!"

At that moment she disappeared behind the screen in the corner of the room and lit a miniature floor lamp shaped like a palm tree, from whose top gushed a pale greenish light. She began dressing slowly, phlegmatically. Her silhouette was bending on the screen's hemp walls in a strange sacrificial rhythm. I stood silent, absorbed in the apparition she had become. Then suddenly her voice came drawling:

"No . . . until Leo's death we lived elsewhere, outside of Sofia. It was only after God took him away that I moved in here."

"Why? So that you could wait for the criminal to arrive . . . and fornicate or commit a new crime?"

"I see that you heal yourself with gall."

"Did you sleep with him?"

"Yes!" she cried out, and it was as if she burst a boil inside of me because I felt relief.

"Here?"

"Here—never!"

"Where then?"

"Everywhere. Is that what you want to hear? So what if I slept with him . . . after all that misery I was in . . . he offered me a hand just before my complete downfall."

"And you fell right on top of what he offered you."

"Stop, it's getting dirty!"

"We breed in dirt, we thrive in it, and we turn into dirt when we die. That's why my tongue is dirty."

Her silhouette froze, as if it became embedded in the screen, and an abrupt silence engulfed the *tableau vivant*. Then a groundswell rose from the corner, it surged, and her voice came wailing, as if from an old record:

"Leo was getting worse . . ."

Her silhouette left its cover. She appeared dressed in wide male clothes, pants and a shirt, a scarf around the neck, and a black belt with an elegant silver clasp.

She lit a cigarette with a languid movement of fingers touching lips, performed especially for me. She advanced lightly and somewhat indifferently toward the cabinet, slid open the small glass door, and took out two crystal glasses and a gourd-like bottle containing a thick black beverage, poured some in the glasses, added the same amount of cream, topped it off with vodka, stirred the mixture with a tiny silver spoon, came close, and offered me the drink with the words:

"White Slave."

I was familiar with the drink, but it was only then that I learned its ingredients. I took a firm swig, and immediately a sheaf of potent alcoholic fumes rushed into my chapped nostrils and whetted my senses.

"It's invigorating . . ."

She took a sip of the enchanting drink, inhaled cigarette smoke deeply, and went on:

"After Leo was gone, he offered that I move to Sofia and come live here, provided for . . . Alone . . . with the nightmare."

"He bought you as bait for the trap."

"I thought he had a sense of guilt—that they caught you while he got away."

"You live here alone, I wonder why? Because of a secret plan? Or maybe not that secret, and not so much a plan but a perverse desire. Look around, open your eyes to this whole foul stage design—plush, tassels, screens, wall rugs with odalisques and camels . . . this whole slimy domestic comfort . . . the stage property of his lechery . . . what sort of people are you, he and you, people with meek faces and randy insides . . . This is a proper boudoir!"

I started kicking, knocking down furniture, and I said panting:

"Men don't live in boudoirs, it's where they go whoring, where they fiddle with women's organs. Slug comes here to relieve his glands . . . There is no way that this bedroom upstart didn't use you like that . . . you are a doll in the hands of a monster that ejaculates semen directly into the mouth of hell!"

The pulse of the silence that descended grew unbearable.

"He raped me!" her voice whined distortedly. "The very first time he brought me here. I resisted, but this infuriated him, aroused him even more, he started thrashing around and then he violated me. He fell asleep as soon as he came . . . I got up, I was out of my mind. I found a bottle of gasoline under the sink and poured it over the bed. I set it on fire and left. Apparently he jumped up, gathered the burning bedding, and threw it off the balcony. I saw it happen with my own eyes as I was leaving the building. He never laid a finger on me again."

She lit another cigarette from her old one and fixed her eyes deep in the wall:

"He owned up straight—that he had bought the crime scene intentionally . . . the trap in which sooner or later you were bound to fall."

"I saw him today . . ."

She was silent.

"He took me to the bathhouse and poisoned me."

"What?"

"What you heard. He treated me to poisoned wine."

"And you?"

"I—nothing! I am in his way. I know the truth and can use it to destroy him."

"What truth?"

"The truth about what happened here twenty years ago, here, in this damned place."

"He poisoned you and let you go?!"

"I ran away."

"How did you know where to find me?"

"It doesn't matter."

She waved her arm to dispel the cigarette smoke winding around her.

"Tell me the truth."

Sadness took over her face. The sadness had a favorable effect on me because I felt sympathy and said, "First you tell me what happened to you after they took me in, and to Leo, and everything . . ."

"Slug went into hiding immediately. He was afraid you'd turn him in. He orchestrated his disappearance—he joined the Young Communist Underground, started distributing leaflets. He threw a paving stone at a policeman and fled into the woods. This happened shortly before 9 September, and it was already obvious where things were headed."

"And you?"

"I left town. I couldn't stand the looks of the neighborhood gossips. My belly was about to grow big . . . I began wandering from place to place."

I think she started sobbing, took a handkerchief to wipe her nose, and then she grew quiet, lit a new cigarette, and went on:

"One day he turned up . . . in uniform, an officer in some special unit . . . he confirmed the truth."

"The truth?!"

"The prosecution's official story . . . that you killed the jeweler with the gun with which he had wounded you, and because you had been wounded, you weren't able to escape, and they caught you at the crime scene."

"That son of a bitch . . . And you believed him?!"

"It sounded probable, but I was fighting with the thought that . . ."

Suddenly she fell silent.

"That what?"

"That you're a murderer."

"A murderer—never!"

"Then who killed the Bijou?"

"He did."

"Slug?"

"That's right!"

"What do you mean . . . why didn't you tell me, why didn't you ever write?"

I was silent.

"You didn't send a single word . . ."

"It didn't work out to spill my heart . . . in a letter."

"No?!"

"No."

"Why not?"

27

It happened a long time ago, during my very first year in jail. I became friends with a guy my age who got in at the same time as me. His name was Valentin, from the Sugar Factory neighborhood, and his face was long and twisted, with high cheekbones. He was kind and tender on the inside, but sinister looking and effeminately ugly on the outside. He had a hump and was nicknamed Scraggy. He walked about as if he didn't belong here but was from some planet of his own . . .

We started talking, sharing things. He was serving time for the murder of his stepfather. He had busted the guy's skull with a piece of rail, which he had accidentally dropped from the balcony. It had slipped out of his hands while he'd been trying to secure the guardrail.

A rumor started, however, that it was no accident at all, that Scraggy had been keeping a close watch on his victim so he could do him in . . . other rumors spread as well—that he was raped by this same stepfather, and then, after his mother had passed away, he became his lover and did him in out of jealousy, and other such nasty insinuations, which were passed around in whispers. But I paid no attention to them and judged the man based on what I saw for myself.

I felt good in his company, a strange and infectious feeling. We almost always sat together in the cafeteria so we could talk. People started dropping hints and talking behind our backs. One day during meal time Lumpy—a fat, greasy goon, a wrestler at fairs who'd broken the neck of another of his kind, for which he was doing time—comes over with his personal slave, a rachitic gypsy. They stand behind Scraggy, and the rachitic gypsy pulls out a sheet of paper and starts reciting at the top of his cacophonous voice a love letter in verse—beautiful, indecent words, openly sexual, almost pornographic. The gypsy was illiterate, but he had apparently memorized it and even rehearsed it. Later we found out it was a love sonnet that Valentin had written to a certain male or female "O." In any case, while the rachitic one is reciting—and neighing like a frenzied mare when he pronounces certain words and phrases—my friend got visibly sick, and then suddenly his bony face filled with blood. He jumps to his feet and tries to snatch the sheet from the hands of the analphabetic declaimer, but Lumpy seizes him with one arm, topples him to the table, and starts dragging him along it like a rag.

I saw red, my arm flew, and my fork plunged into Lumpy's nostrils, deep inside his face, to the end of the tines . . . I turned it, twisted it, and pulled it upward with lightning force so that even his cartilage bobbed up. I come to my senses and realize that I'm holding in my hand a crooked fork with ragged nostrils. I didn't even have time to be disgusted because Lumpy yelled murder and lunged forward to crush me with his body, but I met him with a vigorous series of straight punches, which turned his face into a bloody diaper. He collapsed to the ground and bellowed like a slain ox. They took him straight to the hospital, and they threw me in solitary confinement, where I spent three months on bread and water, on a bare concrete floor and in total darkness. I never saw them again . . . they had scattered them in other coolers.

It was then that Van Voorst advised me not to write letters, especially love letters, because apparently there was a plot, and they were looking for a pretext to provoke me to a fight so they could kill me. Time went by, and the trauma of this incident turned into a principle—not to write any letters—and a principle is what makes a man.

28

"Whose Sofia address was that from which you mailed the letters to me . . . whose was it if you actually lived here that entire time . . . whose was the address where I was supposed to write to you and spill my soul . . ."

"He gave it to me so he could monitor what you were writing."

"So I was right not to respond."

"It was right for you, not for me."

"Why?" I said abruptly. "Tell me. I need to understand."

"What?"

"You."

"Lev, tell him the secret so he gives you the antidote . . . to hell with the stone, you live!"

"The antidote is a bluff. There is no such thing . . . a lie . . ."

"The lie, Lev, hides in . . ."

She started to ramble pathetically. I nodded somewhat mechanically, as if I were listening and silently participating in the conversation, while a nagging thought was building up in my head, and it built up so big that it was about to explode my skull from within—the thought that she too was playing a part, that she is part of a larger, parallel scheme, that she's playing the double game of live bait, herself on the hunt. I felt betrayed, dried out, drained, depleted, wasted, empty, violated . . .

Suddenly, mechanically, I started walking backward and passed into the kitchen. She followed me, timidly at first, then aggressively. She was saying things I wasn't hearing. Raging centrifuges were howling in my ears.

I was taking ever more decisive steps backward, and she was right there, narrowing the distance. I was looking and seeing through her, as if with X-ray eyes. Her face was changing rapidly, and suddenly panic rather than worry flitted across it. This happened at the exact instant when I felt my back against the kitchen window, the very same window through which I had once broken in.

My arm slid mechanically behind my back. I put my fingers on the frame. It gave way and opened. Icy shivers ran down my spine, and my face distorted into an eerie smile. Then, following some deranged impulse, I closed one eye and winked at her.

She froze on the spot. Then it was as if some invisible hand vigorously shoved me, and I felt my body, clad only in a tank top, relax and fly backward and downward out the window . . .

My ears carried away the blunt shriek she gave and the striking of a clock—it was two o'clock in the morning.

I had wished to taste my death, but it was not to be.

29

I don't remember how I fell. I remember how something suddenly rattled me abruptly and loudly, and to my misfortune I found myself caught in some copper wires and a frozen-stiff, white bed sheet. I thought that death was embracing me and I settled back for a second, but then the freezing cold cut into me, and I realized that it was not death at all but a most banal idiocy.

I was entangled in the clotheslines of one of the lower floors, and I was now hanging in the air three meters from the ground—all wrapped up and ready for ridicule. I thrashed about until I landed on the ground amid a pile of crates, my lungs in agony.

When I came to and started breathing relatively steadily, I found my head lying in a woman's warm lap. A coat covered me, and her hot breath brought me back to life. I looked at her lips:

"The bride and groom may now kiss," I said, not knowing why.

She kissed me on the mouth and confessed, "Lev, you are the life you just tried to take away from me . . ."

She was exhaling rather than uttering her words. Stock words, as if prepared for an occasion like this one, stolen from the phrase book of some maiden. Her breath was turning into white frost and sprinkling on my face like celestial dust.

"I want him dead . . . I desire his death!" Tears streamed down her flushed cheeks like snowflakes on hot glass. "After a night out drinking, on the way back from The Hoof restaurant, he fell asleep in the car as soon as he parked it in the garage. He just dropped drunkenly and dozed off. It occurred to me that I could leave him like that in the car with the engine running and finish him off . . . I couldn't find the strength."

"I will kill him . . . he killed me first!"

She raises me kindly and tenderly, as though she is worried I will shatter as I get up. I sit next to her on the crates, put on my coat, and embrace her.

"Tell me about Leo."

"Leo is no longer with us. He's just a grave now."

"Let's go see it!"

"Now?"

"I don't have much left to live."

"Let's get away from here."

"Where?"

"Abroad, there are doctors, they will cure you. We'll need money . . . I'll get some from the beerhouse register . . ."

At that moment of utter weakness, futile hopes overcame my senses. I still don't know how I could have bought this idea of a way out. Man is nothing but debris; he's weak and sour.

"No!" I said and suddenly fell quiet so that I could accentuate what I was about to say next. "I have it . . ."

"What?"

"The stone!"

"The stone?"

"The diamond!"

"Where?"

"In the Orlandovtsi cemetery!"

"What?"

"In the jeweler's grave."

She looked at me in astonishment, as if I was out of my mind.

"In the coffin!" I declared firmly.

Right then, the yard gate screeched chillingly. Someone's pudgy silhouette emerged from the darkness. Then came a hysterical shriek, like a spluttering squeal:

"Hold it! Don't move, you murdering pervert."

"Quiet, quiet, comrade Zhivkov . . . It's me . . . It's all right, everything's fine, there are no murderers here. I dropped my scarf out the window, and we're looking for it now. I was trying to hang it on the clothesline, and as I was putting on the clothespins it fell . . ."

"I see, girl . . . but you scared the bejesus out of me. I heard a racket and then screaming and I thought— maybe it's that deviant guy, they've been looking for him for months now, the one that rapes women in a rain jacket and with a paving stone . . . All right, I'll be heading in, then, because it's getting to be the small hours. My shanks are all frozen, and my sex life is kaput."

"The doorman, Temel Zhivkov, a lecher and gossiper, always snooping around . . . Let's get inside."

"Where?"

"Upstairs . . . You're going to have to tell me the truth!"

I was looking at her, listening to her voice, and only now realizing how little of her had been preserved in my memory.

30

We sat on the old, sagging couch under the wall rug with the camel, and I began to tell how Slug and I heard her signal and went down the rope, how Vlad Lyolyushkin caught us and what happened after that, how Slug shot him and then shot at me so that he could take the figurine and do away with me as a witness, how they started breaking down the door on the outside, how Slug ran and . . .

"And then," I say excitedly, "I stand leaning over the dying jeweler and watch his face contort in agony. Then my fingers mechanically unscrewed the figurine, and suddenly an exquisitely black carbonado diamond fell into my palm. I couldn't believe my eyes and convulsively clenched my hand into a fist to make sure of the physical presence of the stone in my hand."

She took hold of my wrist, squeezed it violently, while I looked at her and went on:

"At that moment, a sudden sense of panic overcame me. They were already breaking the hinges on the entrance door out in the hallway. It was a matter of seconds before they would find me in front of the expiring body with loot in hand. They could shoot me on the spot. I needed to get out immediately, through the window, and they were already rushing in. I looked around the room—I needed a place to hide the diamond . . . suddenly I heard a sharp wheeze and my eyes stopped wandering and fixed on the face of Vladivostok Lyolyushkin, who was expiring before me. His jaw gaped convulsively, and then completely instinctively I dropped the stone into his mouth and closed it with two hands. The agony lasted mere seconds—the dying man swallowed, wriggled as though struck by thunder, and came to an end. At that instant the front door came down on the cement floor with a crash, which launched me straight into the kitchen, and then directly out the window and . . . darkness. I came to in the hospital guarded by policemen."

"Did anyone ask you about the stone?"

"No. Nobody suspected that there was a stone, that there was a third person, that there was you. There was just me. I go in to rob him, the Bijou finds me, shoots at me, wounds me, a fight ensues, I take the gun from him and shoot him. End of story."

"And the lie worked."

"And it became the truth, at least for you . . . at least for twenty years."

"So there was a stone after all . . ."

"Yes, and it was buried together with its stonecutter."

We fell quiet, as if each of us had started counting silently to infinity. All of a sudden the doorbell rang, then it rang again, and I gave her a questioning look.

"That's the postman," she uttered calmly. "He always rings twice."

"The postman?"

"The messenger, a soldier on duty who delivers telegrams from Slug. He has no faith in telephones—he believes he's being tapped. He sends me telegrams, which I'm supposed to burn as soon as I've read them."

She left the room, and after a brief conversation with the soldier returned to the living room with the telegram in hand, which read:

"Moths in the closet. Act according to plan."

"According to plan?!"

"Lev, understand . . . I'm just a weak woman stuck in an impossible triangle with two men. One of them is one too many—let's get rid of him!"

"How?"

"It can happen when we come back from the cemetery with the diamond and before we set off for the border. Slug will come here at exactly seven-thirty in the morning to catch us still in bed because," she had headed for the window, "I will have moved this vase with the dry autumn leaves from one end of the windowsill to the other. This will mean that you've spilled the beans, and he can come to collect his precious nugget."

She took hold of the vase, moved it as required, and then added in cold blood:

"We'll put an end to him here tomorrow morning. Let's go now!"

I looked at the clock. It was three-fifteen.

I'm feeling nauseated, but not then—I'm feeling nauseated now, as I write about all of this. I need to breathe deeply, here, I'm breathing . . . it's passed.

31

I bent over the toilet bowl trying to throw up, until finally fresh bile spurted out my mouth. I stand up and breathe deeply to stop the agony. I stretch my arm to flush the toilet. I squeeze tightly on the chain of the toilet tank—a metal chain with a brass weight at the end. I snatch it violently and rip it off. I twist it around my hand. I take another deep breath. I tuck away a piece of *zift*. I move my jaws around and gather some saliva in my parched mouth. I go out, leaving the guttural roar of the toilet tank behind me.

I remember that while I was lying in her lap down in the yard and coming around after my fall, I caught a glimpse in the dark of the crooked frame of a bicycle ditched among the pile of empty crates. We set off for the Orlandovtsi cemetery on it.

Wrapped in a homespun blanket reeking of moth balls, we were advancing slowly and arduously. Her body jolted against me. I was pedaling with all my muscular might, which was fading fast. I had to stop from time to time to gather strength in the deepest and iciest night I had ever seen.

At one point it becomes impossible to advance further on the bicycle because of the ice and the crisscrossing tracks, so we chuck it and continue on foot.

We duck into an entryway to get some rest, we breathe into each other's faces for a while huddled together, and then she says:

"That's it . . . I can't go on, I have no strength left . . . I'm staying here . . . you go on . . . by yourself!"

"I can't either . . . I can't by myself!"

We remained like that a while longer, deep in silence, as though waiting for a miracle to happen that would transfuse energy into us from somewhere. Then my gaze started to clear up, and I notice in the dark the outlines of a baby carriage:

"Come on, you'll ride in a carriage."

She looks at me as if I'm raving mad, but then she realized what I was talking about and barely managed to say:

"Hold on . . . you're out of your mind!"

I had already grabbed her in my arms and was seating her in the baby carriage, or rather shoving her in, and we flew out of the entryway. I pushed frenetically until I tripped and fell face down on the ice. I breathe heavily and look up to see the baby carriage dancing on the ice. Then suddenly it veers to the side, slams into a snowdrift, and capsizes.

Ada screamed, jumped to her feet, and gave a truly childlike laugh. She throws snow at me as I walk toward her, her face beaming with happiness.

"Hey, it's not me but you who needs pushing!" she says as she prods me vehemently in the back to move forward.

We drag along on foot. I look back, driven by a sudden impulse, and I observe a lonely overturned baby carriage sticking out of the middle of an ice desert, thrust there as it were by an evil Moira, and I think to myself, "I hope it's all over soon."

She knew where Leo was buried, but in order to reach the jeweler's grave, we needed a plan map of the cemetery or someone to tell us where to go. I knew the exact plot and number of the grave, but I didn't know where it was situated in the overall layout of graves in the Orlandovtsi metropolis of the dead. I had asked a friend from the slammer who got out a year ago to inquire at the cemetery administration and write to me. And that's what he did.

In addition to a map, we needed a shovel or an engineering tool to break up the frozen earth. The gravedigging crew would have a shovel and a plan, so we needed to find them at that time of the night.

"I hope you have enough strength," she whispered in my ear and suddenly her voice hardened. "Do you?"

"I do until I die!"

32

The entrance door is roughly nailed together, and hanging on it is a piece of bent sheet iron which reads in capital letters "GRAVEDIGGERS: HEATED QUARTERS." Below that, handwritten in oil paint, it says "ENTRANCE FOR STAFF ONLY."

The sooty window is glowing dimly. Croaking voices are coming pell-mell from inside, followed by sporadic slaps. I knock, the door opens on its own, and I peek in.

A sharp odor of rubber boots, galantine, and granuloma poured over my face. A momentary silence fell inside. And what do I see—rough faces, as if scraped with a file, lips cracked to bleeding, hair matted to foreheads, fists wedged into armpits, bloodshot eyes, pulsating musculature caught in T-shirts. Men immense and angular like volcanic masses. Gravediggers, seven of them, gathered around a red-hot blazing potbelly stove, playing Guess Who Slapped You a moment before we catch them.

The Wired Radio Outlet was feeding classical music into this communal, domesticated hell.

"Good evening, good people!" I say in embarrassment.

"Hey, you, what are you doing here at this hour!" a hoarse, angry voice rends the dirty air.

"Who would be the chief here?" I ask politely.

"That would be me, Petar Raichev, deputy-chief, the chief isn't here."

Petar Raichev was an ungainly, large-boned man, wide in the pelvis and narrow in the shoulders, his face sulky but soft, as though overboiled, and his eyes shining with undeniable class consciousness. His head—large and warped like a giant tuber—was caught in an oily elastic net, which gathered his anemic hair in a heap.

"People, and you, Raichev, help! We got lost in the dark," I appeal for human kindness.

"Man, it's the middle of the night, and this is a cemetery, not a roadside inn!" Raichev declared unruffled.

"Exactly! We're looking for a grave," I say visibly feverish.

"A grave? And who is to lie in this grave?"

"No, listen, we're looking for an existing grave."

"Now! And what's the rush?"

"A medicine woman sends us to bury in it a personal item belonging to our late father, immediately, because otherwise something bad is going to happen."

I borrowed the medicine woman idea from folklore.

"Yes, it would be fatal. We're brother and sister," Ada adds with a dramatic falsetto in her voice.

Petar Raichev looks us over carefully, studies us from head to toe, his face stretching backward and freezing in a mask of astonishment. He says:

"It's the first time I encounter a case of such . . . ," he is looking for the right word, "wacky nature. Fatalism, medicine women . . . give me a break . . . Aren't we all communists . . . Huh, aren't we?"

"Good people, gravediggers!" Ada appeals in turn. "Understand, a curse has been cast over us, an evil hex . . . We didn't keep our father's will, and we had to come here at midnight to bury in his grave a personal item . . . three feet under."

"Hey, you, filthy bourgeoisie," Raichev cuts us off, "it's a one-dog night outside, the ground is frozen solid. Where should I call—the police precinct or the madhouse?"

"Why such heartlessness?" I go on, "We haven't done anyone any harm, and we are moreover fully cognizant of what we're asking. We've been sent here precisely because it's difficult and not easy to dig, because we're talking about an ordeal of an extra-corporeal nature, a probation of the spirit and such."

"Good people, we beseech you, help!" she despairs. "The help won't cost you anything. On the contrary, we'll give you some money to buy yourselves a drink."

Ada pulls out a wad of money. The deputy-chief gravedigger looks greedily at her hands, as I continue in the same humble key:

"Give us some advice . . . give us a shovel or a pick-axe to break up the ground."

"We can give advice, but not a shovel or a pickaxe, definitely not!" Raichev brushes us off. "We use these shovels to earn our keep. They are exactly seven in number, and we're responsible for them."

"We pay what it takes," says she.

"We return what we take," say I.

"Do you see this Wired Radio Outlet right here?" the deputy-chief bulges his eyes at us. "Well, tomorrow, after the 'Deeds and Documents' broadcast, every one of us leaves this place with shovel and pickaxe over our shoulders."

Petar Raichev then looks hungrily at the wad of money and decides: "You two seem loony to me. And here order and supervision reign. This is an occupation as old as the world, an honest occupation, not some unlettered drudgery."

While Petar Raichev is stringing proud words about his line of work, Ada takes a rubber band from her hair, slowly rolls up the wad of money, and fastens it. She tosses this lump of money into Petar Raichev's hands. He catches it and, turning to the rest, says: "We divvy up equally."

He tears off a sheet from the pile of newspapers stacked together with pine kindling next to the blazing potbelly stove and says to me:

"The address—plot, row, grave."

I write down the numbers, and he in turn sketches a map of the sector where the grave is located and tells us:

"There you go! Now get lost before I report you to the authorities, before we scoop you out with our shovels, before we break up your bones with mattocks, before we stretch you out over there on that machine for drying cat skins—the one the apprentice Solakov created—before we start beating you like death drums."

I look in the indicated direction and notice the machine in question emerge from the fetid murk in a corner of the room. The machine for drying cat skins was an odd contraption made of two old jagged spades and a worm-eaten mattock. Their metal parts formed something like a trident from which hung wire ropes and strings on which a cat skin was stretched to dry. I realized that the machine consisted of digging instruments, and deep inside me a decision was reached to act coolly.

"I came out of prison today," I say with a fierce look, "and I'll return there for murder and violating a corpse if I don't leave this place with that machine."

I untwist the toilet tank chain, make a noose with it, and lunge at Petar Raichev. Catching him by the throat, I start to strangle him, while he's squealing and kicking.

"We just ran out of money," I yell at the gaping gravediggers, "so make your pick—Raichev or the machine! I'll pluck his head like a chicken's and leave him here so you can dry him."

I tighten the noose, and Petar Raichev croaked and tumbled to the floor, which tightened the chain even further, so that he started kicking and gurgling far more expressively than the first time:

". . . take it . . . let go . . ."

"Hey, you illiterates, didn't you hear?" I roar at the confused crew of gravediggers. "Bring out the item, as one man—right away!"

They started to move slowly, like animals wakened from hibernation, and as if by command, they lifted the machine and headed outside. When the group reached the threshold, I loosened the noose somewhat. But just then one of them, in tight leggings, stocky and knobby like a cannonball, charged forward, blocked the entrance with his body, and cried:

"No! Over my dead body. I invented this machine, I assembled it, I operate it, I will be going with it to an art show. No!"

"Solakov . . . give up the machine!" Raichev wheezed.

"Ingrates!" grumbled the gravedigger-machinist. "This machine has only done good by you. We earn our *rakiya* with it and do well altogether, because it's a first-rate means of production and a means for making fur collars, but moreover it is a means of artistic expression . . . Isn't that right, Raichev? You said it yourself!"

At that point, the gravediggers threw the machine for drying cat skins out over its creator's head, and upon hitting the ice, it broke apart before his sorry eyes.

I release Petar Raichev, and he starts breathing freely.

"Solakov," I say cheerfully, "don't be sad, be a merry apprentice. You will invent a new machine, a better, nicer, more efficient, and a far more expressive one."

Then the Wired Radio Outlet interrupted me and Exact Time announced the hour. It was 04:30.

Without further ado, I grabbed a couple of the machine parts—a mattock and a spade—and Ada and I left the premises of the gravediggers' heated quarters to continue our journey through the cemetery wilderness, leaving behind us deputy-chief Petar Raichev with a lump of money in his hands to stare after us not knowing what exactly had transpired.

33

We first went to pay our respects at Leo's grave. The alleyways had turned into glass from the cold, and I treaded with great insecurity, carrying the parts of the machine for drying cat skins over my shoulder. We were advancing slowly and arduously, speechless, having reached unmentionable depths of mutual loathing.

Suddenly she stopped and turned to me with a feverish face. I also stopped and heard her voice scattered by the dull howl of the wind:

"His first name was Leonid . . . and thus Leo," she said and lowered her eyes.

"Leonid." I digest the news.

This revelation, made right there, seemed to me quite inappropriate and not without a secret design, a circumstance that filled me with foreboding of an unanticipated dénouement.

We easily find the spot.

"Over there, behind the thick tree," she says, pointing in that direction as she steps aside to let me go first.

I approach the grave, stand in front of it, and my stomach turns over from what was there for me to see. I staggered backward in surprise and leaned on the age-old tree.

The grave was fresh. A wooden cross was sticking halfway out of a pile of crumbly soil. Somebody was buried here—the obituary specifies—yesterday! And the death of this somebody sharply changes the course of this whole lame story.

The obituary says: "The twelve black years since the death of her firstborn son Leonid (1944–1951) also finished his mother Paraskeva (1922–1963). May she rest in peace."

I turned around and met her eyes with the ferocity required to show how I was seething from these wholesale lies. I headed toward her and grabbed her by the throat, but my fierceness melted, and instead of hurling her dead to the ground, I said:

"Where have you brought me? . . . Why am I here? . . . Who are you!"

"I would have been a mother, and you a father, but we lost our child before I gave birth to him. I conceived from you before the robbery, you remember, don't you?"

"Twenty years that's all I was doing—remembering!"

"But after you went to jail, I started getting by in beerhouses and hovels, and I miscarried. I really wanted this child, and I didn't have the heart to tell you the truth. I was afraid I'd lose you, and I decided to lie."

Silence and an ominous blizzard howl.

I stare at her closely with eviscerating eyes. I stare at her, the greatest variable in the equation of every life at stake—the female one. And she speaks:

"I needed a grave where I could bring you when you got out . . . and I found it. I was here the other day, I laid fresh flowers and . . ."

"And if the mother of the Leonid resting here hadn't died that same day, the whole scam wouldn't have come to light."

"Yes, the whole thing, the whole scam came to light . . . that's all there is. The rest is as you know it . . . it's just that it wasn't in the stars for Leo to be born in the first place."

I learned from her then that after a few years of dissipation she was sent to a correctional labor camp for the morally corrupt. That is where Slug found her and made arrangements for her to be released under his guardianship, with the express understanding that she would dance to his tune.

"Bullshit!"

I raise an arm to waste her, but suddenly out of the dark jumps Slug, gun in hand. I freeze, ready to laugh at the stupid trick they had pulled on me. Wasn't the slug-major supposed to show up in this whole black comedy, not here and not now, but tomorrow morning, at the crime scene? He had obviously been following us the whole way; the moving of the vase contained a signal hidden from me but clear to him.

She looks at me cold-bloodedly—without any surprise at the antagonist's sudden appearance. Then she goes to stand behind him, like the archetypal accomplice.

I try to chop them up with a sharp look as I speak: "The vase with the dry leaves! Who are you really trying to get rid of, him or me? Or maybe both of us!"

"Bummer!" squealed Slug, "wrong guess. Now about face and forward march to Lyolyushkin's grave!"

Something clicked in my head—Slug could shoot me in the back and take the map of the grave's location. I stop, take the piece of paper out of my pocket, study it carefully, then I roll it into a ball, swallow it pointedly, and say in turn: "Bummer!"

Slug looks at me with a growing frenzy in his eyes and says: "Lead us to it, or I blow your brains out and extract the map together with your esophagus."

I approached him and he darkened. I spat in his face and started leading them with the clear idea that whatever happened he wasn't getting any diamond.

I violently squeeze the brass weight and walk ahead, plowing the icy air and blazing a trail, while they move a step behind me. I start to wander about in order to gain some time, which gets on their nerves, but then I realize that I am more likely wasting time and think to myself, "Go on, Moth, get to the end of this lame story already."

34

Moonstruck marble frames a deserted, barely legible grave. I stick a half-broken shovel into the age-old ground and start crushing it—at gunpoint. The metal rings out, and the stiff-frozen earth barely gives way.

I am ready to drop.

Slug also starts digging with the piece of mattock, because dawn will break soon, and I couldn't manage on my own to scoop out the heavy dirt that lies on top of Lyolyushkin.

We take turns. Now the major is digging, I'm throwing out the soil, and she's holding the gun. He harbors no suspicion about her, which means they are in cahoots and I will be sacrificed . . . I already have been!

I am silent. I plod diligently, and I try to guess from their faces what is destined to happen. Slug is swinging the pickaxe and doesn't notice how the gun takes to vacillating and starts pointing now at me now at him. So I decide to tease him:

"Slug, do you get the trick she's turning?"

"Dig and stop babbling!"

"The bitch moved the vase so she could bring you out here to dig as well, because there is no way I can manage to scoop out all the cubic feet of earth lying on top of Lyolyushkin. We're holding handles, and she's holding the gun, get it?"

Slug looks at her and stops digging. With the help of the pickaxe he jumps out of the grave, approaches her, and reaches to get his gun back, but she points it firmly at him and says:

"Don't come near or I'll shoot . . . get back in and dig!"

And he tells her in feigned high spirits, "Are you kidding me . . . don't play with fire or you'll get burned . . . you're a shrew and a shithead . . . come on, shoot!" And he coolly moves closer to her.

Her arm starts to shake and slowly drops, her knees bend, demons start darting across her face, and her body begins to tremble, overtaken by sudden frailty. The major takes back his gun with one hand; with the other, he lets go of the pickaxe and whacks her such a slap in the face that he knocks her to the ground and leaves her lying there unconscious. Then he lifts the pickaxe, leans over the grave with the pointed gun, throws the tool inside and screeches:

"Dig! Things just got rough!"

I dig, poke, rake. I act assiduous. Otherwise he'll do me in. Beyond the horizon, the dawn is filling up with light and is about to crack, and the jeweler is lying a meter beneath the blow of the mattock.

Some time went by and finally the metal hit wood and I cry out:

"Here, you rabid weasel!"

The major leans over and peers into the dark to see what's happening down here where I am, lest I beat him to it again and snatch the diamond first.

A cloud covers the pale moon, and I say to him: "Look, you creep . . . here!" and I throw dirt in his eyes.

The major, blinded, starts rushing about. Ada jumps to her feet and shoves him in the back. He staggers forward and falls down on top of me. I put a wrestling hold on him, manage to get his gun, and fling the firearm deep into the night. He recovers, however, grabs the shovel, flings it at me, and knocks me down with a blow in the back. I fall facedown, he kicks me in the kidneys, and then with bare fingers he starts digging at the bottom of the grave until he manages to rip off a rotten plank.

I was already on my feet when the cloud unveiled the pale moon and the coffin yawned before my eyes like a ripped paunch. The inside turned out to be empty—no jeweler there, just a small silvery urn with an inlaid inscription that read:

"Life turned into ashes. The ashes acquired a diamond body. The body of carbon Man. You, brother, who art here—what are you made of, ashes or diamond?"

Slug opens the urn, I rub my eyes vigorously, and what do I see—inside there is just grayish dust and nothing more. I burst into hysterical Homeric laughter and blow the dust about in all directions. The two of them look at me as if I've gone mad.

"What, what?" she asks perplexed.

"Speak!" he seethes.

I pull myself together and explain:

"The inscription points to a proverbially simple physicochemical fact. A diamond and a handful of ashes are both made of carbon, only differently structured. If subjected to the appropriate thermal treatment, ashes form diamonds."

"So what?" growls the major. "The diamond was burnt to ashes, is that what you're saying?"

"I'm saying what you see for yourself. Vlad Lyolyushkin was cremated, and the diamond that was in his stomach came to light and someone appropriated it, some expert on the 'physics of ashes.' This someone decided to philosophize on the issue and composed the inscription."

At that instant, Slug bolts upward trying to jump out of the grave, but I pull him by the legs and he slides down. A battle of life and death ensued. I managed to untwist the chain wrapped around my wrist, swing the brass weight in the air, and bring it down on Slug, then again and again, until he fell lifeless with a busted skull.

Vengeance makes one feel good, even very good, but only for a brief moment, and I think to myself, "I wish this moment could last." But it was not to be.

With a last effort, I start desperately clambering up the sides of the grave. I pass the shovel to Ada so she can pull me out, but she snatches it from my hands and hits me with it across the face. This was the last time I saw her. Even now, her living image is standing before my eyes—with a crooked shovel in hand and a bluish face.

Was she gripped by some fear that the vengeance that had occurred before her eyes inside the black earth's womb would catch up with her as well—I don't know . . . Actually, only God knows.

Here follow kaleidoscopic stars, I fall back into the grave, and then suffocation—an unbearable, deadly suffocation is pushing down, squashing me until I completely lose consciousness. She was burying me with soil.

I come to, but not fully, just enough to realize I had been buried alive. In my mouth I feel icy fingers smelling of weapons lubricant.

"Slug!" I think to myself dreamily and lose consciousness again . . .

35

Suddenly a lightness descends upon me. I feel my chest unfettered and I realize that someone's strong arms are removing the weight of the earth pressing down on me. Fingers, crooked like a pair of tongs clasp me by the wrist and someone's inhuman force starts to drag me out. It hauls me up and opens my eyelids.

I take a look. Above me hovers the volcanic face of Petar Raichev, deputy-chief gravedigger, who says something to me with a breath reeking of soggy cabbage, but I can't hear, and I think I've gone deaf. He lifts me up, grabs me by the waist, and starts dragging me down the alley toward the gravediggers' heated quarters.

My senses return somewhat, and I see the moon dive into a cloud and vanish quickly. Then the shadow of a black widow flitted in the shimmering murk and seemed to wink at me.

36

I come to my senses sprawled on the wood floor in the gravediggers' heated quarters. Raichev's heavy mouth, as though full of raw innards, descends over me and asks:

"Who are you, brother?"

"A stranger who's eaten an inordinate amount of shit."

Raichev fell silent, searching for the right words, and when he found them he said:

"The bigger the shit, the lesser the damage—a forensic fact!"

"Petar Raichev, are you messing around with a person on his deathbed?"

"Not at all!" he looks at me concerned. "Let me tell you a story so you'll realize that the world around is not set up all that bad."

He sees to it that I'm lying comfortably, puts a pair of misshapen work boots under my head, sits next to me with crossed legs, and begins his tale.

"A few years ago, a gravedigger named Kalcho worked on our crew. A former septic truck driver, sacked on disciplinary grounds by the Hygiene Commission in connection with the following incident. Kalcho is married, but his wife is a horny bitch who sleeps around. He's so green-eyed jealous he's about to explode. She goes out with girlfriends to have Turkish white fudge. Kalcho follows her, and indeed, the bitch goes to a sweetshop, but there aren't any girlfriends there, only the pastry cook Bozduganov, who gropes her, young and wild, with the drive of a boar due to all the chocolate, get it? Well, the whole adultery comes to light when the pastry cook takes the bitch to his place to fornicate. He lives on the ground floor in an apartment building on Opulchenska Street, next to the house-museum of our leader and teacher Georgi Dimitrov. While they are copulating, Kalcho hatches a retaliatory strike with the septic truck he uses to earn his living."

Here Raichev makes an emphatic pause. A lightning smile flits across the gravedigger's face, and he goes on with his story.

"The next day Kalcho is working around the neighborhood like crazy, fills his truck all the way up, then drives straight to Opulchenska Street, throws the hosepipe over the pastry cook's windowsill, and pumps the whole load into the apartment. That's three tons of fecal mass. Kalcho gets in the truck and splits, acting as if shit wouldn't melt in his mouth, if I may put it this way to a man on his deathbed. But then the police get on his tracks and he's caught. The investigation finds the presence of two and a half tons of inert excremental matter inside the apartment and another half a ton pulverized all over the walls and furniture. A lawsuit is filed, and the pastry cook appears in court to testify. The prosecutor asks him:

"'So now, comrade Bozduganov, you come back home after a hard day's work to get some well-deserved rest, you open the door, and what do you see?'

"'Shit,' the victim says imperturbably.

"'Yes, sure, but didn't you feel nauseated, didn't you throw up?'

"See, the prosecutor is trying to establish both the moral damages sustained, and the material ones.

"'No,' says the guy. 'I didn't throw up one bit.'

"'How so?' gawks the prosecutor.

"'Just so, comrade prosecutor,' the pastry cook says coolly. 'Had it been a turd or two, one might throw up, but in the face of two and a half tons of shit, one remains impervious to nausea.'

"The point is simple!" Petar Raichev sums up. "The bigger the shit, the lesser the damage . . . the moral damage, that is, not the material one."

I smiled involuntarily, grew thoughtful, and then I say to him:

"Petar Raichev, you seem to be a good man, as earnest as Lenin. Your stories aren't lame, and you also saved me from an untimely death. That's why I'll share my final wish with you, because my time is up soon."

"Speak!"

"I want you to get the chunk of *zift* from the pocket of my coat, which I left at the grave. I need to refresh the taste in my mouth before I die."

"No problem, I'll go get it."

It's butt warm inside. The cold is gone. The night dies out, and I lose consciousness.

37

I come to abruptly, as if frantically running away from death.

Exact Time on the Wired Radio Outlet announced that it was 06:45. A sprightly voice prompted us to engage in spontaneous physical exercises and started leading the workout:

"Do it, one, two, three . . ."

I look around—I'm still lying on the floor in the gravediggers' heated quarters. Then suddenly, dark like a hailstorm cloud, Varadin Lomski's face leans over me. Behind him peeks Zaharin Smyadovski, a sore, red boil between his eyebrows, holding an inkwell and a pen in his hands.

"Write!" shouts the craggy fathead. "Write your confession, put down everything, expose yourself fully in front of the law's vigilant eye. Spill everything from start to finish, the way it was, so it's here in black and white. Make it visible like on film for the people's judgment, before you're a dead man, you sponger and recidivist, defiling the open spaces of our motherland."

38

And thus, not fully restored, I start writing this confession in the gravediggers' heated quarters so that the black-and-white truth can come to light, so it becomes clear that all along everything was not what it seemed to be, but something completely different.

I feel it, the end is near, the black widow's wig shows behind the door, and I think to myself, "It's time I put an end to this dissolute ordeal of mine here on the earth's crust."

The poison has already penetrated deep into my bone marrow, dulling the quick under my nails. I can no longer feel my fingers. I do have the sensation, however, that styluses of some sort are piercing the joint of my right shoulder, and now, as I move my hand while writing these lines, it squeaks annoyingly like the rusty door hinge of a decrepit neighborhood outhouse.

Exact Time announced the hour, 07:00. The first sergeant came in with a large, roughly carved rubber stamp in his hand and tells me threateningly:

"That's it, boy . . . you're done for! I'll affix your seal now, and you no longer exist, you're gone—like a scab forever scratched off."

"I told the truth . . . anything kept to myself is an untruth!" I wink, but not at him—at the darkness pulsating in the corners of the room.

The fathead's eyes grow fanatical, gaping like two parallel deserts, and in them glitters a tempering that citizens tend to acquire when engaged in perpetual physical exercise. His speech is flamboyant, his words carry the breath of fresh mortar. His brain is a gray lump of tallow, which doesn't let go of the concept that everything in this world is a cheap lie if you don't set it down in black and white.

"Sign!" he yelled and some bubble burst inside him.

And with the last drop of ink in the pen, and with my last muscular powers, I, citizen Lev Kaludov Zhelyazkov, sign this document, hereby enclosing all material evidence in my possession—her letter, the postcard, the fake eye. There is nothing fake where I'm headed, nothing is lame there, and the prosthesis is unknown.

The first sergeant starts flailing like a rickety windmill and slams the seal over my signature with seismic force. Then he collected the confession, inkwell, and pen, and left me forever.

As if by some miracle, a blank sheet of paper slipped out of his hands without his noticing and landed by my side. I now realize that I am really not quite done telling my story, so I pull out the indelible pencil stashed in the small pocket of the gabardine to put an end to this story on the last empty sheet of paper I have left.

I spit on the pencil and write.

39

Dawn is breaking. Petar Raichev emerges from the texture of the morning with my coat, seats himself next to me, gives me the *zift*, and I say to him:

"Like a night moth, death beats in our faces, and we can't grasp it!"

"An interesting metaphor!" he notes. "It reminds me how in the army one time during night maneuvers we boiled some beans out in the open. In the morning, we find the cauldron full of drowned moths. The fire had attracted them. I had stuffed myself with pests without my knowledge, and it made me so sick that I refused to eat for a long time. Then a doctor told me that the bean and the moth are made of one and the same substance— protein—only one protein flies and the other sprouts. And strange as it may be, this fact of natural science brought back my appetite."

"The moth and the bean are like ashes and diamond."

"Which is which?" the gravedigger asks himself.

"I'm about to find out!" I utter my last words and fall silent forever.

I watch the dawn apply itself to the sooty window of the gravediggers' heated quarters.

"The day is calling!" Raichev declared and left me for good.

Exact Time noted 07:15. The Wired Radio Outlet played the familiar signal and the program "Deeds and Documents" came on.

The announcer's voice, deep and solemn, was saying:

"On this day, 22 December, in 1920—three years after the Great October Revolution—the Eighth Soviet Congress unanimously approved Lenin's plan of grand historical importance for the electrification of Soviet Russia.

"Under conditions of unprecedented economic ruin, the Congress delegates—starved, tattered, brutalized—are sitting in the chilly and barely lit hall of the Bolshoi Theater in Moscow, listening with bated breath to Lenin pronounce the prophetic words: 'Communism equals electrification plus Soviet power.'

"The Congress resolution reads: 'Workers and peasants will approach the fulfillment of the plan with watershed determination and wholehearted selflessness, and at all cost, despite all hardships, will report in time its implementation in the life of the country.'"

"Deeds and Documents" ends, repeating its signal.

The gravediggers all jumped out of their plank-beds and lined up to welcome the historic inevitability of the coming day. Then they flung sharp pickaxes and shovels over their shoulders and set off for their eternal seedbed to bury into the ground the previous day's crops.

Post Mortem Scriptum

Now, utterly fatigued, I bite at the *zift* as if it were a dead-man's pacifier and tear it open with my aching teeth. A gorgeously corpulent carbonado diamond pops out of the *zift* and rolls into my palm. I feel its coolness, then hold it up in the air and let the light of the dawning day impregnate it with newly born photons. I drop it into my frigid mouth and swallow, then roll over and end like the lame story that I was.

And when dusk falls again, a black widow with a bony face will silently flit across a fresh grave that will read:

"Moth, who lived fortuitously and died accordingly."*

<hr>

*I copied Stalin's dictum, which appears at the beginning of this confession, from a plaque hanging on the wall of the gravediggers' heated quarters.